Chasing *Shadows*

Elizabeth Tyson

Chasing Shadows
Copyright © 2024 by Elizabeth Tyson.

MILTON & HUGO L.L.C.
4407 Park Ave., Suite 5
Union City, NJ 07087, USA

Website: *www. miltonandhugo.com*
Hotline: *1- 888-778-0033*
Email: *info@miltonandhugo.com*

Ordering Information:
Quantity sales. Special discounts are granted to corporations, associations, and other organizations. For more information on these discounts, please reach out to the publisher using the contact information provided above.

Library of Congress Control Number: 2024919758
ISBN-13:   979-8-89285-331-6   [Paperback Edition]
                    979-8-89285-339-2   [Hardback Edition]
                    979-8-89285-332-3   [Digital Edition]

Rev. date: 10/28/2024

ACKNOWLEDGEMENTS

*F*irst and foremost, I want to thank my amazing man for always pushing me and believing in me during this journey and this process. Many, many times I have wanted to quit and give up, and most of those times, I did. But I didn't do it without hearing, "You are selling yourself short. You got this, babe." It's been a long process, but we've done it. *Chasing Shadows* is real, babe. Thank you for always being there for me and cheering me on. I love you more than there are words in this book.

Secondly, I need to thank my father. No one ever thinks of the important stuff until they are old enough to, and I think that I finally reached that point. I love you, Dad. Thank you for giving me life.

I would like to thank my mother, and my mother's memory. If she were here, she would be—what we call today— "foaming at the mouth" for Olivia and Jackson, and she would be my *biggest* advocate. Her and I never saw eye to eye when I was a child, and yet, I know that if she were to make it to my adulthood, that things would have been exponentially different.

My best friend, Kiahya—you have been on this journey with me from the beginning. You hyped me up when I wasn't motivated, you helped me keep writing, my friend. It wouldn't be as good without my first alpha reader.

So many people have been with me from the beginning of this process that it's hard to pick and choose who to acknowledge. But, please know this: if you and I speak on a daily basis, you were a part of it, too.

Thank you, the reader, from the bottom of my heart, for helping make my dream come true. I hope you love Jackson and I hope you love Olivia even more.

DEDICATION

*T*his one is for the parents who have *survived*, in every sense of the word. Life hurts more than it helps, and sometimes we need a little escape.

TRIGGER WARNINGS

Dear Reader,

Please be advised that while Chiefland, Florida is a real place, any, and everything else in this book, is entirely a work of fiction. All characters and any aspects of plot are completely made up from my imagination.

There are mentions of: self-harm, sexual assault, death, murder, thoughts of suicide, depression, anxiety, explicit sexual content, and marijuana and alcohol consumption by minors.

There are very difficult topics that are discussed, and only enter with utmost abundance of caution. Your mental health matters.

PROLOGUE

Jackson

Since the first step onto this long and lonely road, I knew my time would be limited. I vowed to never marry, to never father children. I was given a second chance solely to follow orders. A soldier. And the breath in my lungs, regardless of what was asked of me, was...enough.

For a while.

They say life is all about choices. I had always thought that life was about bullshit things like time or love. For a long time, I was a disciplined man that prided myself in all the carefully selected choices I'd made, especially when I was following orders. I had a higher power to answer to.

Until Olivia Hayes.

Everything I knew went out the door when it came to her. She was an experience. And hope. And love. And I saw my future with her. I experienced the way that her love slowed my time down and made me wish for more, I knew that it wasn't bullshit—life being about time and love. And I knew I'd made a good choice when I chose to let myself love her and be with her and cherish her time.

But...pride comes before a fall. And there are so many fucking choices that I regret.

It wasn't long before I realized that Olivia had a gift. An incredible capacity for love and forgiveness, despite the ugly and disgusting things that human beings can do. She loved me, and my blood tainted hands. Despite the darkness that encompassed me, and the death that followed, she *loved* me. Not everyone in this life gets to experience that.

Before her, I had always known death was coming quick for me, but after her…I'd begun to think that the finality of death wasn't something I should feel comfortable hurling towards. She gave me something I'd never had. And suddenly, being a soldier, following orders, being just a piece of a massive machine wasn't enough anymore.

Before her, my fuel to make the right choices was to keep *me* alive.

After her, it was to keep *her* alive.

She was a mystery at first, and I quickly fell in love with the forbidden. I didn't know who she was before my heart began to beat for her. Even after I learned who she was, even after I put her and myself in danger, I chose to love her and let her continue to love me.

My choice, though, wasn't meticulous. I didn't plan to love her. I didn't *want* to. But, I did.

I was so madly in love with that woman that I would have reached in my chest and plucked my heart out if she needed one. She was a good choice. Even if it meant that they would take my life. And I've never had one regret about any of the choices that I've made. Ever.

Then…then it was all shot to hell. That death that I'd so often anticipated had arrived. When her tear-filled, wide, amber eyes were *pleading* with me to stay, begging me not to leave her…I had never felt so much regret in my life. I'd regretted ever choosing to love her, because I knew that the pain that caused her to scream out for me, the evidence of it running down her face, it was because of me.

I'd hurt her like that.

Because I was taking those last burning breaths.

Because I was going to that forbidden void that I knew wouldn't stay a stranger for long.

Because I was *dying.*

And I fucking hated myself. I hated myself for so many choices I'd made. But there was one that stood out above them all.

I hated myself for loving her.

CHAPTER

One

Olivia

"So, you're seriously telling me that you would not sleep with him if the opportunity came up?" Sadie's eyes are fixated on Landon, my—our—best friend. We've been through thick and thin, the three of us.

I grip the open book between my fingers and follow her gaze.

Landon Williams and Ryan Williams, first cousins, their fathers are brothers, both strain under the weights as they lift them above, Dalton Barbara and Kyle Thompson spotting them.

Ryan is Sadie's boy-toy. Quarterback of the Chiefland Indians, full ride scholarship to the University of Florida. Even though he is an asshole, he is pretty. They both are gorgeous specimens; God definitely took his time creating them. From the golden hair to the perfect smiles, to the toned muscles and smooth tan skin. Especially when they are slick with sweat lifting their weights. They wear these stupid little headbands that are made of sleeves cutoff from t-shirts, to hold their shaggy sandy hair away from their face, and black basketball

1

shorts. T-shirts without the aforementioned sleeves, cut out and exposing their sides.

Landon would be the perfect match for me. He is kind and sweet, but, *he's my best friend*, and I'm not in the market for anything at this stage in my life. I've worked tirelessly for the last three years for my future, to go to Los Angeles for school. There's an apartment that I'll be sharing with two other girls, we've all already put the down payment for the place, we just have to wait for the current tenants to be out of there…and for the rest of us to graduate high school and move in a year.

Although I'm chomping at the bit to leave, I do love my town. Chiefland, Florida is an incredibly small town that has seven redlights. Its food staples are Barbecue Bob's and Ronald's Burger House and it even has a Super Wal-Mart. The population is only about 2,300 but seems to be growing more and more every year with each new RV park that is built.

If I knew that my mother wouldn't come back here and screw up my life, yet again, I would stay. Especially for Nana, but…I just *need* something new. I need to create my own life, for myself, with nobody that I know weighing me down or stopping me or influencing me in any way.

I need to become a new person, and I'll stop at nothing until I've done that.

"He's my best friend, Sadie, and besides, the opportunity has come up, several times, and I'm just not wanting anything serious. Landon is fun and sweet, and I don't want to ruin that." I respond, repositioning my hold on my book and reaching for my cherry cola with my other hand.

The cool bubbles burn my throat slightly as a bead of sweat slides down the back of my neck. Mid-October's heat is making itself known in the only way it knows how.

Blistering and maddening.

Typically, I wouldn't be here in the weight room on a Thursday. Or any day, for that matter. My schedule is very tight, and the only reason I'm deviating from it is because my car is across the street at Chiefland's Auto Shop getting new tires on. My dumbass hit a nail. In three tires, apparently, which is highly suspicious. I think they might just be wanting to upsell or screw me since I'm an ignorant teenage girl. What would I know about cars? All I knew was that the front right tire was flat this morning when I went to get in it for school and I had to have it towed.

Sadie gapes at me like I'm missing something. "I know Landon is fun. Sex with Landon would also be fun." She averts her gaze back to the boys when they jump up and high-five, hooting in the way that high-school boys would.

Why would Sadie be thinking about how fun sex would be with our best friend?

I press my lips together and tilt my head at her. "Sex with Landon would make things serious, and like I said, I don't want anything serious, Sadie. Besides, he's going away for college and so am I. There's nothing wrong with doing what we're doing." I set my Styrofoam cup down and reach up to twist a lock of hair around my fingers.

"And what are you doing?" She lifts her brow at me.

I shrug. "Hanging out."

A scoff and a shake to her head. "You haven't even kissed yet."

I shrug again, twisting the hair around my fingers. "We are literally only best friends." I say matter-of-factly, even though she *knows* that. "And besides, we have, but it didn't go anywhere, because he knows I don't want it to. He's respectful, and sweet, and—"

"That's exactly why you should fuck him, Liv!" Sadie bursts out in a whisper-yell, her torso twists at the waist towards me.

A puff of air shoots through my nose in a pathetic laugh. "It's not happening, Sadie," My head shakes with a smile and I jut my chin toward Ryan, "worry about you and your own Ken doll."

Sadie sighs defeatedly and leans back against the black painted brick wall. "He's a boy, Olivia, if he's not getting it from you, he's going to get it somewhere."

Okay? What a weird thing to say. I don't want to think about who my best friend is fucking. She shouldn't be either.

"So, let him? I don't have a claim on him, he doesn't have a claim on me. We just hang out and laugh. We've had this for literally as long as we've known each other. I'd say he's my best friend." Sadie shoots me an offended glare. "Besides you, of course." I add and wink.

"I just don't want you to miss out, Liv. Landon is hot and kind, and you deserve somebody who will make you smile." As if sensing we are talking about him, Landon finds us on the back wall and smiles sweetly. I return the gesture and drop my hair to add a small wave.

"He makes me smile."

"And I bet you a hundred dollars that he would make your toes curl."

"Sadie." I protest, looking away from Landon to her. She tips her head back and laughs, her perfectly straight and white teeth flashing. I shake my head with a roll of my eyes.

Mercedes Thomas is a force of nature. She says her parents were fucked up on LSD when they decided her name. They wanted her to sound like she is made of wealth but I think she lets that get to her head too often. I also think it humbles her a tad that people call her Sadie rather than Mercedes. She's the center of attention, always. She's funny as shit. Any time I need a pick-me-up, she is the perfect person for the job. She even pushes me to go way out of my comfort zone when I need to. Normally being a wallflower, I'm satisfied just watching other people have fun, but Sadie would never allow me to *not* be part of anything that she's doing, we've been friends since the beginning of elementary school. There's only one year out of all the years and multiple classes we've had together that we haven't been in the same room. And that's this year. The past three summers I've taken extra online classes to get more credits, I've got three more till I hit my twenty-four required credits for graduation, which means I have 4 open blocks that I'm supposed to be working—with the exception of today.

My car isn't finished yet. They promised me by three this afternoon, so I'll still be able to make it to the last half of my shift.

Hence the reason why I'm in the weight room on a Thursday watching Landon and Ryan work out. It's only 1:30, so what better way to bide the time?

"Hey, ladies." Ryan practically coos as he and Landon near us. They both reach up and tug off their headbands, wiping the back of their neck with it. Their golden locks tumble in the most perfect and messily tousled way around their face. Their builds are a little different from each other, Ryan being taller and slender and Landon being a shorter and more filled out, but they look more like brothers than cousins.

"Hey, boys. Y'all ready for tomorrow night?" Sadie drawls as she stretches her legs in front of her and crosses her ankles. Tomorrow night is the Homecoming game. Sadie didn't get nominated for homecoming court, but I don't think it bums her out. She's won queen and princess in the three years before. Senior year is the most relaxed I've ever seen Sadie. She isn't on the cheerleading squad. She isn't trying to be the best of the best in everything. She's just having fun, and I love that she's loosened up for her last year of school.

"Always, baby." Mischief dances in Ryan's crystal blues as he flashes her a smile and drops to his knees to crawl over her legs and give her a kiss that gets way too intense way too fast.

"Oookay, then," I slap my book closed dramatically. "I guess I'll call about my car now." I push off the wall, and bend to pick my cherry coke up. Landon stands and waits with a smile, still blotting his sweaty neck with the cloth.

"Can I help you carry anything?" He asks.

"Nope, this is everything." I hold my soda and my book up and begin to walk past him to the front door of the weight room.

The sun shines bright in the blue sky, immediately beating on my face as we step out into the open air. As seniors, we don't have to follow much of a dress code, but I've never been one to show my skin, and I'm grateful that my clothes are the one thing that Sadie never gives me hell over. I'm comfortable in my jeans and t-shirts, even in Florida's damning heat.

I pull out my phone from my back pocket and dial the tire shop. Once connected, I press the button for speaker phone out of habit. The little shop girl's nasally voice drones out into the air and she immediately knows it's me when I greet her. She dully informs me that they aren't ready yet, and completion will be more like four.

Lovely. I might as well call into work.

"Hey, it's alright. I've got something I have to do so you can just ride with me. I'll drop you by there when it's time." Landon offers with a bright smile. He drapes a sweaty arm around my shoulders and guides me to his truck, both of us hopping in and buckling up.

We sit in comfortable silence as we drive. I've been working so much lately, though, that I'm too tired to say anything, anyways. We've ridden together without speaking countless times. I'm probably more comfortable with him than anyone else in the world.

Regardless, my comfortableness with Landon doesn't outshine the feeling of unease when I realize where exactly this little excursion is taking us.

Pole Cat.

A mostly-canopied and narrow dirt road that has one intersection and each end spits you out into four different parts of Chiefland. Homes are scattered about but it's mostly comprised of farm and cattle land. The end that we got on starts behind ACE, the only hardware store in town, about two blocks away from the high school. Landon has yet to tell me what exactly we're doing on the infamous dirt road, but the sinking feeling in my gut tells me that it's only trouble. The only reason people go on Pole Cat is because it's not patrolled and people can get away with whatever they need or want to.

This...perplexes me, because Landon has always been known as a slavery to safety. He's the one that stands up to bullies for other kids. He's the one that makes sure other people get home safe after parties. He's the one that checks on people when they are sick and shows up with soup and movies or whatever their ailment requires. I know that Landon would never, ever force himself on me, but...that sinking feeling is telling me that the possibility is not entirely impossible as we inch closer to whatever the destination at a turtle's pace. My mind is in the gutter, but it's only reacting to the warmth pulsing through my veins.

His silence doesn't help the matter. This is unlike the Landon that I know, he normally *never* shuts up.

He leans far away from me and his left hand's fingers prod his temple as his right hand's knuckles starch against the black wheel. I know the intersection is closer when we pass a dilapidated shack that's almost reclaimed by the earth and I can practically feel my pulse thrumming in my neck.

I'm not comfortable.

He knows me better than this. He knows I wouldn't be okay with this.

And then he finally speaks, snatching my attention directly to him.

"Whatever happens here, don't get out of this car." His tone is one I've never heard from him, and it pushes me further into the deep end of the what-the-fuck pool.

I can hear the whooshing of blood in my ears as I feel the car park and watch him jump out, practically skipping away. His posture a considerable difference than his demeanor only 10 seconds before. My eyes follow his destination—a man, one of considerable size with black shaggy hair, leaning against a black car. It's old and black, and shiny.

I thought Landon's car windows were tinted, but apparently not enough as I lock eyes with the stranger. The most vivid pair of green eyes that peer at me through thick black lashes holds me in place is as if they were made of pure power. And I wish more than anything that I can say that I've been awestruck this way before...but I can't.

I'm absolutely frozen.

With fear or admiration of the stranger's beauty? Perhaps equal parts of both. His eyes don't leave mine as his lips move, saying something to Landon. Landon turns and looks back toward me, shrugs his shoulders, and waves me off.

My hands rub against the knees of my faded jeans, trying to rid the perspiration from them, but it doesn't slow my racing heart.

What the hell are we doing here, Landon?

The stranger doesn't look away, the intensity of his expressionless gaze almost offends me, as if I've done something for him to stare at me. Landon proceeds to speak, his hands doing most of the talking for him. It seems as if he is trying to stand in front of the man to block him from looking at me, but he is considerably smaller—in height and width—and all it takes is a tilt of his head or the raise of his chin and his eyes are back on mine.

We've only been in this staring contest for a couple minutes but it seems like hours already, and it's pumping my adrenaline.

Why is he staring at me like that?

He listens to Landon speak, and takes a wad of cash as Landon fishes it out of his pocket. The first time since we've arrived, he looks down to his hands and counts the money. A lot of money. Twenties and fifties and hundreds.

My eyes drop as I follow his to the money in his hands and I take the small reprieve of captivity to take in the black ink etched into his skin on his fingers. Skeleton bones. There's a mystical whisper of shadows that cover the skin surrounding the lines of the bones and they travel up his hand and wrist, cutting off at the crease of his elbow. His tan upper arms are halfway covered by a black t-shirt that fits snug against his skin. He almost needs a bigger size, judging by the way he fills the fabric. The muscles in his hands and forearms flex and stretch as the bills travel from one hand to the other.

Landon presses his hand against the black paint of the man's car and immediately pulls away when the man cuts his eyes to him. He doesn't even open his mouth for his message to be conveyed. Goosebumps spread across my skin as if he threatened me personally.

Once he's finished with the stack of money, he pockets it, fishes out a pack of cigarettes from his other pocket. He listens to Landon talk about whatever nonsense he appears to be talking about and pulls a cigarette from the pack, slides it back and forth across his lips, settling it in the corner of his mouth, and lifts the lighter, torching the end.

And then he looks up slowly, seizing my breath.

It's a strange phenomenon, being held captive by a set of eyes. And it's extremely unnerving. Almost to the point that I want to squirm and wiggle away, but that small voice at the back of my mind tells me that it won't deter him.

The sheer willpower that is seeping off of him can be felt through the small distance *and* the car door. He pulls on the cigarette and his skeleton fingers pull it away, the smoke softly puffing out.

I read somewhere that the way to make an alpha back off is to not reek of fear, and I refuse to appear like a small and weak and fragile little girl.

So, I keep my eye contact.

Until Landon realizes that we are in a staring match and he stands in front of the stranger, cutting off our wordless battle. Those green eyes avert downward to Landon, and he says something to him. Landon looks back to me, and then back to the man. Whatever Landon says in response must not be savory, because my heart leaps to my throat when the man wraps those skeleton fingers around Landon's neck and slams him against the side of the black car.

Without a thought, and within a half a second, I'm out of the car and running to Landon's side.

"Hey! Stop! Get your hands off of him!" My voice sounds distant to me but I'm sure I'm yelling. My steps are nonexistent but I'm sure I'm getting closer. By the time I'm standing next to him, his feet are inching off the ground. The smell of cigarettes hits me like a ton of bricks, but something else too.

Something *more.*

Coffee? Leather? The unmistakable male scent clouds my head until I see the color drain from Landon's face as he claws at those skeleton fingers.

"It's okay Liv," Landon croaks out, struggling to take a breath. "I'm okay. I just have a smart mouth. I shouldn't have said anything, man, I'm sorry." However, Landon's assurances fall short when he can't even mouth another word.

My hands fly to the stranger's forearm and I tug as hard as I can, trying to pry him away. But I'm small and weak compared to the massive build of this strange man, and I don't know what else to do except stomp my foot and yell at the top of my lungs. "I don't know who the fuck you think you are, buddy, but this is my friend you're hurting and you need to let him go!"

Finally, as soon as I feel like a bull with steam billowing from my ears, those striking green eyes find mine and stop me in my tracks.

A wordless command and I'm a hostage.

Even my breath is at the mercy of his silent order.

This close, I can make out his features better, and…he is unlike any man I've ever seen in my life. His strong square jaw is set with determination and his eyes are even greener as they stare down at me through a fan of black lashes.

And the intimidation is much more real this close, only a half a foot away. His cheekbones are high and perfectly positioned, his nose exquisitely strait, and his lips… I've never wanted to reach out and touch a stranger's lips before to see if they are as soft as they look.

My curiosity of him repulses me.

My eyes find Landon once more, his face blanched and his eyes beginning to shut. My nostrils flare in desperation and my jaw clenches as I regain control of my body, fighting whatever voodoo that this dangerous man is comprised of. I straighten my shoulders out, mustering every bit of strength I can manage.

"*Let him go.*" I grit through my teeth.

That earns me one response—a raised thick brow.

My heart pumps once.

Twice.

Three times.

And then Landon lands on his feet with a thump, coughing and sputtering, clawing at his neck. The tall stranger steps aside as Landon stumbles and struggles to get his balance behind him.

"Incredibly stupid." His voice matches the intensity of everything else about him and the hair on my neck stands on end. He shifts toward me and Landon finally stumbles around him and up to my side, too quickly for me to inquire further about what I know to be true. My knowledge of my stupidity is engrained in me. My mother never let a day go by without making sure of it.

Before I turn to assess Landon, the stranger's eyes fall to where my hands pull my best friend into me and I finally yank my attention away.

"Thank your girlfriend, Superstar, she's got bigger balls than most of the grown men I know." Dark shaggy hair tumbles across his forehead as he turns to his car and yanks on the door. "And she's the only reason why you still have breath in your lungs. Good luck at the game tomorrow, kid."

Landon leans against my shoulder, still clutching his neck. I struggle to support him and find those green eyes again.

Captivating.

Alluring.

Fucking dangerous.

And they are gone before I can even begin to process how they make me feel.

CHAPTER

Two

*W*arm sweat clings to my forehead and upper lip like makeup. August and September was relentless, but these last few heat waves in October have been brutal. The bodies around me and the lights beating down on us create this oven of perspiration and flesh.

Friday Night Lights.

Chiefland Indians vs. Dixie County Bears.

Homecoming game.

Other than the state championship itself, the homecoming game is the holy grail of all the games that should be won for the Indians. My last three years of high school, when the coaches were picking the games, they would pick an easy team for us to beat for homecoming.

This year, it wasn't our pick. And what are the odds of our absolute rival being our homecoming game opponent?

Normally I wouldn't be concerned with who is playing who for any reason. The only reason I go to any of the sports games on Friday night is because Sadie asks me to. But tonight...there's cops everywhere to protect the peace. There are fights that break out every time that Chiefland and Dixie plays, and a couple times people have died.

It makes me nervous to be in an environment where I can't make sure I'm safe. I'm not in control anymore and it's not what I'm used to or even anything that I *like*.

And the heat doesn't make it any less nerve-wracking.

Sadie convinced me to wear a pair of short khaki shorts and a white tank top. I was able to talk her out of makeup or doing anything with my hair other than putting it up in a messy pony tail. But I still thought I might as well be naked when I looked over myself in the stand-up mirror in the corner of her room. She met me in front of it and assured me I was "hot," pointing out, unnecessarily, that we were matching, and that made me feel a little less…naked. Even though she's about four sizes smaller and its undeniable that the shirt I'm wearing is Sadie's. It doesn't even reach my waist.

Everyone around me takes their turn stealing glances as if checking if I'm actually still me.

I'm still Olivia Fucking Prude Ass Hayes. If you take a picture, it would last a lot fucking longer.

My boobs practically hang out of the top of the low-cut fabric and my thighs rub together stickily as I shift from leg to leg while the band finishes their rendition of The Star-Spangled Banner.

Sadie nudges me gently and I find her crystal blue eyes, quieting the noise in my own head. She's always had a knack for doing that with her reassuring smile. Everyone sits down after the prayer over the teams and the concrete is rough against the back of my legs.

Fuck. I wish I was wearing jeans.

After a few announcements, the game commences.

Landon is easy to find, blue and gold jersey wearing 87 on his back. He is also easy to lose as he ducks and weaves through the black and red jerseys. Sadie squeals as Ryan tumbles over a couple massive boys and fumbles. A sound of disdain bellows from our student section. Turnover.

Kickoff, catching, passing, turnover.

Or whatever the lingo is. By the end of the first quarter, I gave up trying to keep up with the score or who had the ball and I pulled out my phone, opening the book app that I downloaded last week, specifically for times like this. Sadie has scolded me, and quite honestly, the entire school has picked on me, for bringing actual books to games. Whether it be football, basketball, baseball…by the middle of it, I'm lost in another world within the pages.

So, problem solved. Now I look like every other teenage person running amok. With my nose in a phone during times where I'm supposed to be present.

But it seems like I only can get two pages in before its halftime, and Sadie is tugging my arm, pulling me off the concrete bleachers.

"Where are we going?" I call after her, but she doesn't answer me and we push through a crowd of people down the fence in front of the track.

And then we are on the track.

And then we are standing on the edge of the field.

"Sadie, what the hell is going on?"

"Listen, Liv," Sadie turns back to me, halting us right on the track behind the benches on the sidelines. The cheerleaders finish their routine next to us and the crowd is roaring. I can barely hear myself think over whatever the person in the booth is saying through the microphone. It's all happening so fast. "There is a contest. Ryan nominated me, Landon nominated you, the triplets and Dalton and Kyle and all the rest of them nominated their own person. We have to go out here onto the field in a few minutes and participate! It's no biggie!" Her smile beams and her shoulders shrug, but it doesn't give me the grounding feeling I'm used to. I've never gotten hurt from any of Sadie's ideas. Trusting her is all I've done for as long as I've known her.

So why does it feel like I shouldn't trust her in this moment? She knows I don't like attention, and yet, here we are in front of a crowd of people. A contest means judging. The five hundred people at this football game have the capability to judge… whatever is coming.

I yank my arm from her grasp and begin to shake my head, wanting to give in to every alarm and siren pulling me away.

"Liv, I promise you, you'll be fine. Let's go, they are calling for us!"

And away we go, Sadie skipping, and me—the caboose—tripping, after a line of my female peers, all dressed in skimpy ass white tank tops and short khaki shorts.

I've been petrified before.

I've wanted to melt away.

I've wanted to be invisible.

I've been embarrassed.

But never, ever, have I been any of them in front of hundreds of people, all under their scrutiny like I'm bacteria beneath a microscope.

I'm not sure if I'm red for embarrassment or white from panic, but my ears burn hotter with each new thump of my heart.

Each footstep feels like it's on a cloud as I only follow behind Sadie. Her giggly laughter above the roar and cheering of the crowd on all sides of me cloud me like it's playing through earbuds.

I could run away.

I could yank away from Sadie's hand and run to the parking lot and get in my car and drive home.

Except, we are already in the middle of the field, lined up in front of our team's bleachers.

I would be the laughing stalk until graduation.

Breathe in.

Just act normal.

Breathe out.

I can do this. Just stand here.

Breathe in.

What are we even being judged for? Who is the sluttiest?

Breathe out.

It's okay. Whatever is happening is okay, you will be okay, Olivia.

Breathe in.

Look at them. My eyes follow. An ocean of people before me.

Breathe out.

I'm light-headed. My eyes flutter closed but when I feel like I might fall, they fly back open.

Breathe in.

Where are those balls you had yesterday when you stood up for your friend to that... man?

Breathe out.

Unlock your knees. What are we waiting on? Is that roar coming from the bleachers or is it my heart?

Breathe in.

I don't dare close my eyes, again, because I know I'll get woozy if I do.

Suddenly, every muscle in my neck and back lock up and my vision blurs as ice cold water drenches my entire body.

Wet.

I squeeze my eyes to rid the water and look down at myself, my shirt clinging to me, the lace of the nude bra outlined perfectly underneath the fabric. The dark indentation of my belly button contrasting against my skin, visible through the wet white cotton.

Breathe out.

Oh, my God…

What in the super-fuck did Sadie just pull me into?

The squeals of the girls down the line reach me and mix with the uproar of people all around us.

Did my best friend, who knows me better than anyone, really drag me out here so all these strangers could judge how I look in a wet fucking t-shirt? Is this really happening?

The bitter sting of betrayal burns in the back of my throat and my eyes are cloudy again, but this time, it's not because of the water.

I spin in my spot to see a beaming Landon holding a white bucket behind me, his golden hair wet and disheveled. Ryan stands next to him as he places a kiss to Sadie's lips.

"Oh, you are so winning this contest, Liv." Landon's voice doesn't even sound like his as his eyes rake down my wet body and back up. My arms cross instinctively to cover my chest, as much as I can given that there's a horde of people around me.

Stop looking at me like that, Landon!

How could my two best friends do this? Put me on display like this? If this is a joke, it's not funny, and it's the worst joke I've ever been a part of.

I spin back around, the early autumn heat finally warming my chilled skin. The goosebumps begin to dissipate with each passing second. My eyes roam over the smiles and the hollers and the cheers.

And I spin back toward Landon, finding that the rest of the team had done the same thing to the other girls. I spot the visiting team's bleachers and it's filled to the brim, all of them having the same reaction as our side.

Absolutely fucking disgusting. Whoever thought of this deserves jail time. Half of us standing out here aren't even eighteen. This is practically predatory.

"Lighten up, Liv, you are so hot right now. Look, everyone agrees!" Landon closes in on me and when my mouth falls open to speak, he leans in before I can get a word out and presses his lips to mine.

What. The. Fuck.

As quick as the words cross my mind, my hands fly up to Landon's chest and I shove him away. The roaring crowd dips with a soft gasp when Landon leans away from me.

"Olivia, I'm s—"

"No, it's my fault. It was my idea. I'm sorry." Sadie interjects when Landon begins to apologize. They share a soft smile and steal a quick glance at each other. And I want to forgive her that quickly.

Him.

Both of them.

As if it's a dream and I just woke up.

But it's real.

Therefore, absolutely fucking not.

Not while I'm still standing out in front of a mass of people with my two best friends, one of which, who just tried to make a move on me in front of all these people and the other one who pulled me out here for it to be done.

And I'm still fucking wet and half naked!

My head shakes back and forth as I take a step backwards. They are absolutely insane. And awful. Awful friends! More than a decade of nothing but love doesn't, and could never, outshine something like this.

I take another step.

Then another.

And another.

And both of them watching me defeatedly get further and further as I walk backwards off the field.

Once I reach the track, I turn around and continue my trek. My phone and my keys are snug in my back pocket—hopefully my phone works after being waterboarded.

My mind is practically dazed, because literally...*what in the actual fuck just happened?*

Just as I reach the back fence that has a secret gate, my eyes begin to water, and I clench my teeth, forcing myself to wait until I'm in my car, at least. I refuse to let anyone see me cry.

But *damn it!*

My best friends. My best fucking friends. I'm completely humiliated. I've only felt this powerless one other time in my life, I told myself I'd never allow myself to feel that way again. And here I am...doing a walk of shame after trusting my best friends. I should have pulled away on the track the first time, and didn't listen to Sadie when she told me it was going to be okay. It was one hundred eighty degrees away from okay.

Is this what I get for trusting people? Should I have completely shut down when my mother left?

I take a few steps down the path, almost to the middle of the massive concrete wall that was built to shield traffic from being able to watch the football game without paying, and the flick of a lighter snags my attention to the left, over the two-lane road.

And I'm met with the most stunning pair of green eyes, his lips and nose and cheeks being illuminated by the cherry of the cigarette.

My steps slow in response as my heart picks up, the realization of who exactly is sitting across the street from me sets in.

Sadie, and Landon, and the crowd, and the wet t-shirt that I'm standing in falls away.

It's the strange man from yesterday. He sits atop the very top of his car, his ankles crossed over the windshield and his hands resting in his lap. He wears the same attire, blue jeans and a black t-shirt. His hair just as messy as it was yesterday. It'd dark out now, but the stadium lights illuminate his features in the best way.

And those chilling ass skeleton bones on his forearms and hands.

Did he just see the most humiliating moment of my life?

Why was he watching?

What is he doing here?

A mass of questions pop off through my head in a matter of seconds.

His eyes never leave mine, and he never offers a word in the minute of eye contact we share. Sixty seconds is an eternity when you are captive in your own body, stunned to your spot by a set of eyes.

He only wears the same emotionless expression that he wore the entire time we stared at each other yesterday.

My eyes follow his hand as he takes a few puffs of his cancer-stick, and graze up his neck to his lips as he exhales.

I blink once and tears race down my cheeks, with more replacing them. I watch him follow the tear streaks, and the realization that he can see me crying sends my feet stepping one in front of the other until I'm safe in my car, putting as many miles between me and Chiefland High School as I can.

CHAPTER

Three

*S*unday morning, rain is falling.

I can smell the coffee that Nana is brewing but I can't bring myself to get out of bed. I don't have the energy, even though I fell asleep early last night.

In the few times I got out of bed, I managed to grab something to eat. A granola bar. A handful of almonds. A glass of water. Nana tried to ask me what was wrong and what had happened but I couldn't bring myself to talk about it. It was already replaying every time I closed my eyes.

Maybe I'm being a tad bit too dramatic. What happened wasn't that traumatic, in the grand scheme, but it's the principle.

My two closest friends forced me to do something that they knew would make me uncomfortable. They knew that I would never volunteer to go out on the football field during half-time, *half-naked*. They know me that well.

And yet, they did it.

It has never occurred to me to hurt or betray my friends. In fact, the only thing I've ever done is be there for them and stand up for them. My mind throws me back to freshman year when all of the high school was talking about how Sadie lost her virginity over the summer. They all were spreading rumors about her being pregnant or having an STD of some kind. Neither of these were true. So, as her best friend, I defended her every time I heard about it, and there was even a huge scene in the cafeteria where I had to tell a senior that he was a piece of shit for talking about a fifteen-year-old-girl's sex life. Not much longer after that did the rumors continue, and Sadie has thanked me for it a million times since then.

I've never had to jump to save Landon, except for the other day when he was getting strangled by that…man.

After I got in my car at the game, I drove straight home, peeled off those wet clothes, showered in water hotter than Satan's sweat, put on the biggest t-shirt I could find, and crashed between my pillows and blankets. And since then, I've been trying to understand why I feel so hurt. I know they were kidding. I know it was a massive joke. I have a right to be mad, though. They forced me to do something they knew I would hate. Both of them. Like they plotted it. What was their goal? To make me a social butterfly? Give me new experiences? Newsflash. That's what college is for.

I know it's okay to be mad at them. So why do I feel incredibly guilty for it and ignoring them?

Every text and call from anyone from school, I've ignored. A couple people have texted asking if I'm okay. Obviously, I caused a scene by running away like I did, and I am dreading tomorrow because of it. I know everybody is going to look at me like a basket case.

My head lolls toward the window and my fingers reach up absentmindedly to twirl a lock of hair around. I opened the curtain earlier when I woke up to use the bathroom. Despite the rain, the early morning sun casts a beam of light across the foot of my bed.

My room has a full view of the front of our property. Our home is placed perfectly in the middle of ten acres, and all the fields surrounding have some kind of animal in each one sectioned off. It's a long dirt driveway to our house, but at the end of the driveway is another dirt road that goes left, and takes you to County Road 345. We live out by Connor's, so it's not an insane drive when I get off from work.

And nothing is prettier than the rainy sunrise through the line of pine trees at the edge of our property.

My mind drifts from the horrific embarrassment that I endured for the millionth time to the green-eyed stranger that was waiting in the shadows afterwards. Who is he? What business does he have with Landon? Why is Landon hanging around this…this…criminal? I don't even know what he does. What was the money for? And what do the skeleton bones mean?

I have so many questions regarding the stranger that practically hypnotized me with one look. Twice now, I've been graced with his presence, and twice I've found myself entranced, even though it pisses me off immensely. I told myself once before that I wouldn't allow anyone to have any kind of control over me, even if it meant dying alone.

My mind could go round and round about the contest and seeing that man. It doesn't change the fact that it happened. It's time to start moving on from it.

My lungs fill with a large breath and I blow it out as I pull myself from bed. I might as well indulge in some coffee while it's fresh.

I sit on the edge of the bed, my bare feet on a grey shaggy rug, and I tug open a few drawers to retrieve a pair of pajama pants and socks.

My fingers rub circles against my eye sockets, attempting to wipe the sleep away, and I stretch my arms far above my head, yawning subsequently.

I mentally prepare myself for the horde of questions that I know is to come when I get to the kitchen, and I think I'm strong enough to handle them.

The walk down the stairs and through the living room to the kitchen isn't long, however, my steps slow when I hear Nana's hushed giggle and a male voice.

I round the corner to find the back of a head.

Golden shaggy hair.

A blue and white varsity jacket.

My grandma looks up from her position on the other side of the island and smiles warmly.

"Good morning, Lottie! Landon stopped by," she gestures towards him with her mug as he swivels towards me with a soft smile, "he said you left the game not feeling well and hadn't heard from you so he wanted to make sure you were alright. Isn't that so sweet of him?" She sips from her mug and watches us over the brim.

I press my lips together and cut my eyes away, making my way to the coffee pot. I retrieve a mug from the cupboard, and pour the warm liquid.

No sugar, only cream. That was something my mother had engrained into me as a young teenager.

Their silence behind me doesn't affect me one bit as I work to make my cup, and then slowly sip it as I gaze out of the kitchen window over the sink, observing the patio and small backyard that had fallen limbs from last night's storm.

"I think that perhaps I should busy myself. It was good seeing you, Landon!" Nana finally says and once her footsteps fade away, I turn around to face my best friend.

His eyes are sad. Regretful almost. The simple act of seeing the sorrow makes me want to hug him and tell him not to worry about any of it and just move on. But I can't be that naïve.

"I'm s—" He opens his mouth to speak but my index finger raises off my mug, halting him.

"What you did was not okay. Not at all."

He nods once and looks to his folded hands in front of him. "I know."

"And my feelings are incredibly hurt."

He chews on his lip, not moving his attention from his hands. "I know, Liv."

"I just...I can't believe that my two best friends would even concoct something so cruel. What have I ever done to you? To either of you?" My voice finally cracks with emotion, but I swallow it down with a sip of coffee.

Shame. That's what is written on his face.

He shakes his head softly. "It wasn't meant to be serious, Liv. I really am incredibly sorry for how it ended up. For how it made you look." He finally looks up at me and his eyes are pleading. But it's not enough.

"What it ended up being is absolute insanity. My best friends dressed me up half naked and pushed me out in front of hundreds of people to be judged, after I had ice cold water dumped on me. As if I were a piece of cattle or a whore, ready for the picking. I am absolutely dumbfounded by it, honestly. I haven't known what to do or think since it happened. All I can do is relive that moment, remembering the absolute fear of all these people that I don't know staring at me as I'm half naked." I set my mug down on the chopping block and lean against it, my head shaking back and forth gently from the memory.

Those crystal blues are filled with sadness. I chew on my lip as a few silent seconds pass, the pressure of guilt resting on my chest. I'm causing that sadness in his eyes by continuing to ream his ass *after* he's apologized. And I feel terrible about it. So, I decide to change the subject to something that I've avoided thinking about.

My posture straitens as take my mug back into my hand, pulling it to my mouth for a sip. Landon shifts in his seat and unclasps his hands, putting them in front of him.

When I met Landon, I was six years old. First grade had just started and I didn't know anyone, other than Sadie. Her and I had class together and we'd been assigned seats next to each other. It was a couple weeks into school and Sadie was sick, so she'd stayed home for a few days. By the third day of eating lunch alone, someone sat next to me.

It was Landon.

He smiled at me and told me his name, and we've been friends ever since. Sadie, Landon, and I. Ryan and Landon started hanging out more in middle school, leaving Sadie and I to ourselves for a few years. But high school came around, and we were back together like we were in the beginning, plus Ryan, every now and then.

Landon has seen me at my worst. He's stayed over, slept on the couch, seen me throwing up. The whole nine yards. Him and Sadie are the most comfortable people to be around.

So…why does it feel extremely awkward right now having just rolled out of bed? Especially after what happened at the game.

"Landon…" I begin, my heart in my throat. I don't want to hurt his feelings in any way. He watches me with an earnest look. "You know that I love you." I say.

He nods. "I know, Liv."

"But, I—"

"Don't love me in the way that I love you?" He raises his brows in question and my words are caught in my throat.

Oh, no...

I blink several times before being able to form any words that don't sound douche-y. I wasn't going to say anything remotely close to that. I was going to tell him that he can't just kiss me like we're together when we aren't.

He's my best friend. Has been for years. That's all he will ever be.

"What do you mean, 'the way that I love you'?" My question is unnecessary, though. I've suspected for a long time. It's been an elephant in the room for several years. At least since the beginning of high school. I just have tried to...ignore it, thinking he would stop if I didn't feed into it.

"You know what I mean, Olivia. I've loved you since the day I sat next to you in the lunch room. I've loved you. And you've known it." He sighs and his shoulders slump defeatedly as he looks at me with those baby blues. "I know how you feel, though, and what you want. I'm sorry for what happened. I should have never done something like that to you."

My heart twists in response.

"Does this change things?" My voice is smaller than intended. I don't want to cry, but the thought of being without my best friend creates a knot in my throat.

Landon smiles and shakes his head softly. "It doesn't, Liv. You're stuck with me. And by the way," he points at me, "thank you for standing up for me with Jackson."

Jackson?

My brows furrow together, and he elaborates.

"Remember the guy on Pole Cat?" He asks.

I nod slowly, because...yes, I definitely remember the guy. It's an instant decision not to tell him that I saw the very same guy at the football game afterwards. I'm not sure why I want to keep that bit a secret.

"His name is Jackson Wolf. He's…" Landon shakes his head as his eyes wander around, searching for the words.

"He's what?"

"Dangerous."

"Landon, what business do you have messing with a guy like that, anyways?" I sip from my coffee.

He takes a deep breath and leans back in his chair; a defenseless shrug comes across his shoulders.

"I just…need the cash. And Jackson has the ability to help me make it."

"But, why do you need cash? I thought your parents were—"

"Rich? Yeah. Me, too. Hey, can I get a cup of coffee?" He stands from his chair as I nod, gesturing to the space behind me and step aside to allow him room.

"It seems like it's dried up enough, we can go sit on the back porch if you'd like." I offer as he pours into a mug.

My heart is twisting for my best friend. The thoughts race through my mind as I step away from him. As much as I care about his well-being if his family is now without money, the questions at the forefront of my mind have nothing to do with him.

Jackson Wolf.

What an anomaly of a name. It sounds completely made up. As I make the small trek out the kitchen and through the living room to the double French doors, I can't help but think of those green eyes and those goddamn skeleton bones.

The sun beginning to peek through the clouds is already evaporating the dampness off the small concrete area behind the roofed back porch. I take my seat in a wooden rocking chair and sip my coffee as I wait on Landon.

"I want to talk about your parents, but, first, I want to know what you are doing to make money. You're always at practice. I don't see how you even have time to work. And that was…" I pause to take a sip of my coffee. "A lot of money to give to someone." I say to him as he takes the rocking chair across from me. He plants his heels on the bottom bar of the chair and his toes push against the grey-painted concrete, rocking softly as if he has no care in the world.

His eyes stay unmoving, focused on the ground between us. An expression I've never seen rests on his face.

"Landon?"

"I'm a part of something illegal, Liv." His eyes are far away. He doesn't take pride in what he does—whatever it is. That much is evident. I stay silent though, careful not to push too hard. Landon has always been hard to open up, and I want him to feel comfortable to tell me whatever this is.

The faintest hint of a breeze blows by us and the windchimes that he and I hung up in the low-grown tree further out into the yard clink around.

Landon sighs. "It doesn't really have anything to do with Dad running out of money. He's not. He recently found out that him and Sheila are having a baby." He sips his coffee and my brows shoot up.

"Oh…wow." My response is short…but Landon knows why. I don't like his father, Adam. Adam doesn't like me. He's an asshole and he deserves for his son to hate him. He had this old money his entire life and he cheated on Landon's mother, Amy, any chance he could. Finally decided to settle down though, and the divorce took everything from Amy, leaving her in a broke down shack on south-side.

"Simultaneously, Mom just found out that she is sick, and her treatments are crazy expensive." His tone is as even as the Florida horizon and my heart drops to my feet.

Amy is sick?

"Oh, Landon..." I stand to hug him and I wrap one arm around his neck. "I'm so sorry. When did you find out?"

He pats my shoulder a couple times and then takes a deep breath as I pull away to sit back down. His eyes find a new spot off to my right to train to.

"It was just recent. Several months now, I reckon." My mind races over the fact that my best friend has been dealing with this for months and I had no idea. I shift in my seat, pulling one of my legs underneath me and sip my coffee. "Before school started back, she had been complaining about how bad the pain was, and I wanted to find some weed to take her edge off. Ryan said he knew a guy, and...then, I met Jackson."

His fingers run through his messy golden hair and he sips from his mug.

Why isn't he looking at me?

"First of all, I can't believe I had no idea about your mom. I'm so sorry. I should have known."

"I didn't tell anyone. I didn't want the pity."

"But I'm your best friend, Landon. I should have known. Does Ryan know?"

"Ehh..." He shrugs his shoulders and shakes his head. "I've told him once but when I brought it up again, he didn't know what I was talking about so I didn't bother after that."

Ryan has *always* been an asshole.

"That's shitty of him." I say with a scoff. Landon nods in agreement.

I continue. "So, you met Jackson and...he sells you weed?"

Another deep, bracing breath.

"Yes. But, he's also a part of something bigger."

"Like a gang?"

A beat of silence as he seems to drift away to a different place. "I guess you could call it that, but they are unnamed. The only thing they all have in common is the bones. On their arms and hands."

The image flashes in my mind. I remember.

Freaky ass tattoo.

A live army of the dead. Whoever thought of it must be a monster. I nod my head to let him know that I do, in fact, remember.

"So how do you make any money off of him selling you weed?" I hate to keep asking questions and prying it out of him, but the connection isn't there yet, he's barely told me anything.

"Honestly, Liv, I just do anything he asks for. Mainly I sell weed to the other students. I've been asked to rob people. Lift cars. Dig ditches." My blood runs cold.

"Dig *ditches*?"

"Olivia," Landon plants his feet on the ground and stops rocking. My entire body locks when those light blue eyes finally meet mine.

There he is.

My best friend.

The one that can tell me anything.

"What I'm admitting to you could put me, and Jackson, and anything else involved, away for a very long time. I could get in trouble in ways that you can't even imagine, other ways than with the law. It could leave my mother broke and sick and suffering, so I am putting my complete trust in you not to tell a soul. I...I just needed someone to know. I'm doing anything I can for my mother, right now. It's not something that I'm proud of, at all, but I've only got so many options."

A sense of pride simmers in my chest knowing that I'm the only mundane person that knows. My best friend is a bad boy. That's cool as hell. But, it's still not safe, and I don't want him to get hurt. Or worse.

"You know you can trust me, Landon. But...what about school? You have a full ride. You have so many more options than whatever the hell you've gotten yourself into."

"I'm not going to school. I'm staying here with my mom." He still doesn't look away from me. Frozen like a statue.

The Landon that is sitting in from of me is not at all the Landon that I know. It's like he's slipped on some sort of mask in a matter of seconds.

"Landon..."

"*Olivia*."

There's still fight left in me to try to convince him otherwise, but the demeanor of the sweet boy that I grew up with is nowhere to be found. Nothing, absolutely nothing, that I say could change his mind. I know that in my bones as I stare back at crystal blue pools of *nothing*.

"What you are doing is dangerous, Landon...I would worry sick about you all the time." Emotion swells up inside at the thought of this, this...this man and all the things that he sees on a daily basis. How all of it has sucked the innocence and the life out of him.

"I've been okay for the last few months. You haven't worried a lick. I've just concealed this side of me. As a member, you have to put in the work, so work I do, no matter how dirty. This is who I've had to become to survive...this. This life I'm living. And I didn't want you, of all people, to see it." He finally drops his gaze and takes a sip of his coffee. "I may be a cold-hearted fucker now, but I did mean what I said earlier. That I love you. If anything were you happen to you because of your affiliation with me?" A visible shiver rocks through his frame as he looks out to the sky. "That's why Jackson gripped me up. Because I stepped to him. I didn't like how he was looking at you, and I told him I'd fuck him up if he didn't stop."

Surprise bubbles up. "How was he looking at me?"

One shake of his head and then he looks out to the horizon, the morning sun finally rising over the tops of the pines.

"Don't act like you don't know." He scoffs.

I shake my head with confusion. "I really don't know what you mean."

"It's how every guy looks at you, Olivia."

I only stare at him with wide eyes.

"Like he wants you."

A scoff tumbles past my lips. There's no way, Landon must have assumed incorrectly. There's absolutely no way that a guy that looks like...that, was or is, interested in...me.

I'm, well...I'm me.

Plain.

Pudgy.

A nerd. I could go on, but Landon interrupts my thoughts.

"You never think of yourself the way others think of you, Liv. I'm a man. I saw the look. I know what he was thinking. I know I don't have a claim on you but I couldn't bear the thought of you in the arms of someone like Jackson Wolf. Nothing about him or anyone he's associated with is gentle or sweet. Please, Olivia, please, whatever you do, do not get involved with anyone that wears that tattoo."

The warning in his voice sends chills over my skin. Nevertheless, I'm not getting involved with anyone. My plan is set, I have goals and I'm going to achieve them. Getting close to someone means changing my life, and I refuse to do that after how hard I've worked.

"I would never, Landon. I'm not interested in getting with anyone now, or any time in the near future. You know me, my plan is already mapped out." I assure him, but there's no resolve to his features. Still just the hard lines that I've never seen set into his skin. He's being himself in this moment. He's not hiding who he really is, now, and I find peace in that. He's different, but he will always be *Landon*.

"Regardless of all that, I came to make sure that we weren't on bad terms after the game. I've got to go on this trip with Dad and Sheila for the week, so I just wanted to see you before we left tonight."

He notices the confusion on my face and he elaborates.

"Our yearly Gatlinburg trip. We moved it up because of Sheila's pregnancy. Dad didn't want her to travel as she gets more pregnant, or whatever, so, he made it for now."

"Well, how kind of him to do that for her." The sarcasm drips from my voice. "I hope you have fun, though."

"I will certainly try, but there wasn't a chance of that happening if I'd left without knowing if you were mad at me or not." A hint of a grin graces his lips and it makes me smile in return.

"Well, I'm not. Go have fun, best friend. I'll be here when you get back."

And with that, the new Landon stands to hug me in my sitting position, and he leaves me sitting in my chair on the back porch. I sip my coffee, that's now almost cold, and continue to rock, thinking about all the things that Landon just uncovered to me.

Having just rained, the wet heat that Florida normally gives off is surprisingly cool. Autumn is here.

I relish in the cool morning air and am surprised to find myself wondering about those haunting green eyes and skeleton bones.

But it doesn't matter, because I will not, under any circumstances, change the course of my life.

CHAPTER

Four

"*Lottie, pack your things, I'm taking you to Nana's.*" My mother's voice pulled me from my favorite book.

The Notebook by Nicholas Sparks. It was the third time I'd read it. I dreaded giving it back to the school library. I didn't want anyone else to be able to hold it in their hands, and my mother was too poor to purchase a copy for me.

"*Why are we going to Nana's?*" My response was dull and lifeless, but I didn't have it in my fourteen-year-old heart and mind to care about respect for the woman I hated most in the world.

I looked away from her, not prepared for the sting of whatever venom was about to spew from her mouth. She whirled around with a full bag in her hand and snatched the cigarette from her mouth with the other.

"*I don't have to tell you a fucking reason, Olivia Charlotte Hayes, but since you want to be grown and you want to demand that I tell you everything like an adult, I need you to stay with her for a couple days while I handle some things.*"

Translation: I met a new guy at the strip club and I'm going away with him for the weekend on a bender, and legally I cannot leave you in the house alone without an adult, even though you can totally care for yourself.

My eyes rolled so far back in my head it hurt.

"Yeah, whatever." I slapped my book closed.

I trudged to my room and threw some clothes in a pink duffel bag that I'd won at school. Pajama pants, a few ratty t-shirts, some underwear, and I only had one bra—which I was wearing.

Mom was already waiting in the car when I shoved my feet in the black converse that were already six-years-old and were beginning to tear in the soles.

I popped my earbuds in my ears and turned the music up all the way, Breathe Me by Sia blasting through the wires. I never wanted my mother to try to converse with me, it only ever ended badly. If she tried to speak on the way to Nana's, I had no idea. I was lost in the piano track and the melody of the song I'd listened to hundreds of times before. I only hugged that book against my chest as I felt those lyrics in my soul.

The drive wasn't long, only a few minutes. Mom had managed to screw her way into a dilapidated shack not far from Nana's.

When we arrived, the sun was beginning to set and Nana greeted me with a smile. I jumped out of the car and tugged on the wires of my earbuds, and wrapped my arms around Nana, telling her hello.

And as I turned around, my mother was disappearing in a cloud of dust. With no word.

My body shoots up in bed, my neck and hair wet from sweating. It takes a moment for my eyes to adjust to the darkness before I look at my phone on the nightstand and see that it's only three in the morning.

A groan falls from my lips as I fall back against my pillows, my eyes training on the fan blades going round and round.

I hate that fucking dream.

I hate her.

Most times I wish that I wasn't born, but then other times I wish that she would have just given me away. She clearly didn't want me.

I haven't seen her since that dreaded day. I push it out of my mind when I'm conscious, but when I'm sleeping, that lonely little girl in my mind reminds me of what snuffed her out for good.

I was fine when she dropped me off. What bothered me was Sunday evening, the realization that my mother wasn't coming back. My life was better at Nana's. I was fed. I wasn't belittled. And I didn't have Mom's boyfriends staring at me like I was a piece of meat.

But it still hurt.

Even after everything she'd done to me, it broke my heart a different way when she left.

And the Olivia Hayes that I am today was born.

I'm determined.

I'm strong.

Nobody in this world will ever rock my strength the way that my mother did, and I hope I never see her again to see if she still has that power.

Sadie's face pops into my mind. She and Landon are the only ones that know the turmoil I go through when it comes to my mother. She's always been there, and of course I forgave her yesterday when she shoved a coffee in my hands and a bacon, egg, and cheese sandwich from Ronald's. Food is always her apology, and I don't mind it one bit.

I pull myself from between the sheets and trudge to the bathroom in my room, splashing some water against my face. My alarm isn't set to go off for three more hours but, when I have that dream, I can never go back to sleep.

Ms. Dorothy, the owner of Connor's, had asked me a week ago if I could skip school and work all day because she has to take her husband to the doctor, and the other two employees have things that they can't break away from. I don't mind. I'd rather go to work and miss all the sideways glances I got yesterday.

Being that it was Monday, I knew I was going to face many things from my peers because of the football game. I was under major scrutiny. Everybody looked at me yesterday differently than they ever had. I haven't quite figured out if that's a good or bad thing. But nobody picked on me or poked fun at me, and for that, I was grateful.

I'm also grateful for the reprieve that work will provide. Just my cash register, my old customers, and my inventory sheet. And my book.

I just started this series and I'm already on the second book, making me yearn for vampire gods that have magic shadow powers.

The day goes by incredibly quick. Lunch time passes and I scarf my turkey sandwich before another customer can come through the doors. And back to reading I go once I cash them out and take the last bite of my sandwich.

I stand and stretch, lifting my arms above my head and checking the time. My head whips around toward the slivers of window that are visible between the wall and massive Pall Mall posters hanging on the glass.

It's seven at night. One more hour and it's closing time.

I shift my weight to lean against the counter and look at the page number of my book. 567. I read four hundred pages today?

No wonder people call me a nerd.

I roll my eyes at myself and start my closing checklist. Take the garbages out, check the bathrooms, do inventory of the candy at the counter, check the pumps, and I wait to count the drawer until last. By the time I'm done with everything else, it's 8:03 and I lock the door.

It takes no time to count the drawer down and do the deposit, and by 8:30, I'm locking the door behind me, making the small trek to my car.

The sunset illuminates the horizon in a soft orange glow, growing into the most beautiful purples and pinks as it drifts into the night sky.

My life right now is boring, but its comfortable. It's a job that's allowed me to do my school work while making money, and I'm closer to my goal of having money saved up for when I leave for LA.

I'd told myself that ten thousand dollars would be enough for me to have as pocket change when I moved until I can get a job, and I'm about a grand away from that goal. The down payment for my apartment is paid. I'd just need to cover food and bills until I find work, so, continuing to work here until graduation would surely put me past my goal.

My little beat-up Honda Civic would have to stay here with Nana. There's no way that it would make the drive to California, and also...nobody drives in LA, everybody uses Uber or taxis. So, I don't have to worry about vehicle maintenance.

I'm so lost in my thoughts that I don't even realize that there is a black car parked on the other side of the parking lot. Nobody is ever here when I lock up and go home, though. I almost ignore the small and quiet alarm that sounds off in my head.

But a noise stops me in my tracks.

The unmistakable flick of a lighter that comes from behind me, back in the direction of my car.

I whirl in my spot and find him there.

Jackson Wolf.

The green eyes.

The dark tousled hair.

The skeleton bones.

The soft orange glow as he pulls on that damned cigarette. The same as he was at the game, and the day before on Pole Cat.

For a moment, I'm frozen to my spot as all of Landon's words play back in my head about this terrifying man that he works for. All the horrible things he makes him do. He's changed my best friend and I *hate* him for it.

Maybe it's only seconds, maybe it's minutes, but we stand there and stare at each other, too long for comfortability. The angst that bubbles in my belly makes it hard to stand still underneath that emotionless stare.

Jackson smokes an entire cigarette, neither of us moving, neither of us saying a word.

What do I say?

What do I do?

He leans against my car's driver door with so much ease, that you'd think he has no care in the world. I shift my weight back and forth from leg to leg and I twirl a lock of hair around my fingers. They work vigorously to expend the nerves running wild through my skin.

He exhales one last time and tosses his cigarette butt on the ground, stomping it out with the toe of his black boots.

The level of relaxation he has is infuriating. Either say something or do something or leave me the fuck alone.

"I would love to go home at some point tonight, I've been working all day." My words drip with as much disrespect as I can muster.

"Mmm," the noise comes from deep in his throat and I'm surprised when I feel it from my chest to my toes. "Busy reading your little book?"

At first it catches me off guard as to how he knows I've been reading all day, but it offends me even more that he would call my book little.

"You're blind if you think this book is little." I spit back, holding the 643-page book up in front of me.

His eyes fall to it for one moment and then focus back on me.

"There she is," one side of his lips kick up. "That feisty *little* girl that I met on Pole Cat."

Little girl?

Oh, this guy is something fucking else.

I can feel the muscles in my neck bunch up with a defense. Absolutely maddening.

"Wh—Who in the hell you think you are?" I say with a shake to my voice, and I'm not sure if it's out of fear or anger. One snort that resembles some sort of half-laugh and then all evidence of humor evaporates from his face.

"Where's your little boyfriend?" His low and even tone.

"I don't have a bo—"

"Where is Landon?" He booms. It hits me like thunder.

A gaping fish is probably what I look like, my mouth opening and closing, unable to settle on an excuse.

"Don't cover for him, Little Girl. Where is he?"

A snorting, humorless, laugh shoots from my nose and I begin to walk to my car. You want information from me? Insulting me isn't the way to get it.

"I'm *not* a little girl. I don't know where he is, and even if I did, I wouldn't tell *you*. So, please, get the fuck off of my car so I can go home."

I stomp up to his relaxing frame against my driver door and stop right in front of him, clutching my book to my chest. Now that I'm so close, and I can smell that damn intoxicating scent. Those goddamn eyes are boring into my soul, I begin to feel like the little girl he insists I am.

But I refuse to shy away, even if my heart is pounding away.

"*Please.*" I grit my teeth, trying to remain as strong as possible.

He reaches out and plucks my book from my hold before I can stop him and steps back away, causing me to tumble forwards.

"Hey! Give that back!" I yell, wondering what in the hell this guy's problem is. I regain my balance and I almost stomp my feet like a child.

He only steps further away, and I decide my best option would be just to stand by my car door. No matter how many times I ask, he apparently isn't going to just leave because I'm asking him nicely.

He reads the title. "*A Light in The Flame.*" I can practically feel the blood rush to my cheeks. This is not the book that I would like people to know I'm reading.

Then he flips the book, reading the back, and opens the book to the page that I have book marked.

Oh, God.

"Please," I practically whine. "*Please,* give me my book back."

His eyes skim the page, the green emeralds lighting up when he reads over exactly what I know he's reading. A smirk graces those gorgeous lips and he tilts his head, finally raising his eyes to me with a lifted brow.

"Interesting choice of reading material." He chides as he nears me. My hands snatch the book away when he gets close enough and I shove it into my black cloth bag that hangs over my shoulder.

How embarrassing that a stranger just read the same filthy dirty smut that I've read all day. Almost as embarrassing as competing in a wet t-shirt contest in front of hundreds of people.

"Not that it's any of your business. Anyways, thanks for the drop by. I'll tell Landon you're looking for him if I talk to him."

I will.

But Jackson doesn't have to know that. There's a reason that Landon didn't tell his boss where he went, and I'm not going to be the snitch that rats my best friend out. I turn towards my door and look in my back to dig the keys out.

"Mmm," he hums again, and once again I feel it from my chest all the way down to my toes, stunning me to my spot. "I admire your loyalty to him. I admired it from the moment you refused to back away from me...for him." His voice feels like dripping honey with a kick of whiskey. "I even admire it now, after he forced himself on you at that game." This simple statement causes me to whirl around, coming face to face with the enigma himself.

"He did not force himself on me!" I practically shriek, almost shaking with...frustration?

He smirks and shrugs, but doesn't leave his spot, only inches away from me. "That's how it looked from my position, and I'm sure he's told you that he's one of my...employees." Those green eyes are...testing. He's seeing what I might say.

I think back quickly to what Landon said. That he could get in trouble in ways that I couldn't imagine. So, I do the only thing I know how to do. Protect what's mine, and stay silent.

My heart races from the lack of space between us and I think I might pass out when he flashes me a toothy smile, popping one dimple out in his left cheek.

"Still, so loyal. He doesn't deserve a girl like you."

"He hasn't told me anything." I say. I force my feet to move away and when I begin to spin back around, a large hand reaches out and grips my chin, pulling me back to him.

I think my heart might stop when our eyes connect.

"That was your third strike, *Little Girl*. Don't lie to me again." He sneers. The disgust, as well as the threat, in his voice sends chills across my skin.

All the enthusiasm has fallen from his features, and the same emotionless expression appears. I know in my bones that I should fear Jackson Wolf.

But there's a small and nagging voice way in the back of my mind that wants to see what he might do if I push him. I begin to chew on the inside of my cheek and nurse the silence that seems to have that acid churning in those eyes. The last bit of light reflects off his incredible features and I can hardly breathe.

Only inches away, I wonder if he can hear my heart pounding.

What is happening?

Why hasn't he gone away already?

And finally, *finally*, he takes one step back.

And then another.

And another.

And he continues to take steps back towards his car, never taking his eyes off of me.

I don't dare move as I watch him open his car door, but he pauses, his face thoughtful. He rests his arm on the top of the door and lazily points his finger at me.

"Drive safe, *Olivia Charlotte Hayes*." Then he slides in behind the wheel, closes his door, the car hums to life, and he's gone in a few seconds. The purr of the engine fades into the distance, leaving the crickets, me, and my confusing feelings.

Because...why did the way he said my name invoke things I've never felt before? I've read about these...butterflies? But I've never felt them for another person. And suddenly...my hatred for him has become entirely complicated.

I know, deep down, and with every notion of common sense that I have, that I need to do everything I can to stay as far away from Jackson Wolf as I can. But I also know, against every piece of better judgment and my moral code, that it's just simply not going to happen.

CHAPTER

Five

"I'm only saying, Lottie, that it would save you an enormous amount of money to stay here and go to the college at the new campus in Fanning Springs." Nana says with reason. Her back is to me as she washes the dishes from breakfast. I stay silent, minding my attitude, as I scoop a bite of cheesy grits into my mouth. On Saturday mornings, Nana and I usually spend the morning together and eat breakfast.

"Besides, I'm an old woman. I won't be able to do all the farm chores by myself soon. I'll need your help."

I'm not staying in this godforsaken, small-ass, living in the 1800s, damn town. Moving away is all I've ever wanted to do, and I refuse to change my mind because Nana is asking nicely.

"Well, there's plenty of strong and capable boys at the school who need work for their work release. Maybe I can let the guidance counselor know that you're looking for someone." I suggest with the slightest bit of annoyance. We've had this conversation more times than I can count.

She turns the water off and rests her hands on the sink as she looks out the window.

"I am not comfortable with my only granddaughter moving across the entire country," she says, almost timidly, and then

49

turns to me, drying her hands with a hand towel. "Have you ever heard of trafficking? You'd be close to the border. I am not ready to let go of you."

All ridiculous rebuttals.

"Nana…" I say after I swallow my eggs. "I just woke up. I really don't want to—"

"Well, I *do* want to have this conversation, Lottie." She raises her brows and plants her fists on her hips.

Nana's once-black hair is beginning to turn grey at the roots, the only sign of her age. She has the perfect skin, not one wrinkle, not one blemish, and her figure is amazing…probably due to doing farm chores for the last thirty years.

She was young when she was married, before today's "legal" age, at least. Her husband, my grandfather, passed away only ten years into their marriage. Ever since then, she's taken care of this farm and never loved another, as she once vowed.

"I've already paid the deposit on the apartment. I've already paid for my tuition for the first three semesters at UCLA. I can't just…ask for a refund."

I finally look down to my food, pushing everything around with my fork, my appetite suddenly gone.

"I know that its selfish of me, Lottie. But, I'll be alone. And I'm scared of that." She finally admits, clears her throat, and reaches for her coffee cup that's between us in the middle of the island.

My heart twists and pulls. It's a fact that's caused me many sleepless nights. The one thing that I don't want to do is leave my grandmother alone. The only person in the world who has cared for me and been there for me since the beginning.

I open my mouth to tell her that I'll visit on the holidays and every chance that I get, but the front door opens and closes.

"Good morning, ladies of the Hayes household!" Sadie's voice chimes through the hall and into the kitchen.

I sit up and clear my throat and Nana busies herself with the dishes once more. "Good morning, Mercedes, you seem chipper this morning." Nana greets her and turns back to her task at hand.

"Good morning, Sadie," I grumble, trying to move past the conversation that Nana and I just had. I take one more bite of grits before standing to take my plate to the sink.

Sadie stops me before rounding the island. "This was on the front step for you, the mail must have run early this morning."

Plate of food suddenly out of my mind, I look to her hands and find a small package wrapped in brown paper.

Like a gift.

My brows furrow as I set the plate down on the counter and take the package from her. I wasn't expecting anything in the mail.

Nana turns to see what I have and Sadie watches me. "Maybe it's a book you ordered!" She suggests, but I shake my head.

"I haven't ordered anything."

There's no writing anywhere on the outside of the package and it's edges are sealed with clear tape.

"What if it's a bomb?" I ask and look between the two of them. Nana chuckles and turns back to her sink, and Sadie rolls her eyes.

"Just open it, Liv."

I take a breath and slide my index finger underneath one of the flaps, tugging softly. The brown paper gives way and it rips down the front of the package, revealing a...book?

Is this a book?

My brows pull together once more as I pull the rest of the paper off.

A giant book.

"See! I told you that you ordered a book."

But…I did not.

It's the next book in the series that I'm reading. A strange feeling settles over me and I look over the cover, admiring its beauty.

"Gorgeous." I breathe out, and open the cover page to reveal a hand written note.

Olivia,

I think you'll enjoy this one even more than the last two. At least, I hope you do.

-J

I can feel my heart speed up as surprise blankets me.

Nobody has ever given me a book before, let alone a book that I'll enjoy in a series that I'm reading. Only one other person knows the series that I'm in right now, and the thought of who it is practically steals my breath. My mind recalls the image of how small the enormous book seemed in his hands, and the way he looked holding it.

"Are you okay?" Sadie asks and Nana turns around when my silence is evident.

I nod my head, my mind clouded. I close the cover, opening my mouth to speak, but Sadie doesn't let me as she grips my wrist and tugs me toward the stairs, and up to my room.

As soon as we are inside, she closes the door and looks at me with wide, expecting eyes.

"In the entire time I've known you, I've never seen you react that way to something. Spill!"

I take a deep breath and shake my head with the whisper of a smile. "You're never going to believe me, Sadie."

Hell, I don't even believe it. A cold, ruthless, killer like Jackson Wolf...gifting me a book? As if he would even care about such mundane things.

Except, apparently, he does.

And that fact, has me smiling like the idiot that I am.

"Try me." Sadie challenges as she crosses my room and plops down on my futon.

"Well..." I begin, navigating around the mess and wonder where I even should begin.

"Who is it from?"

I settle next to her and shake my head, not sure where to start or what to say, so I just open the cover and let her read it herself.

She skims over and confusion crinkles her features. "Do we even know a 'J'?"

I raise my brows and breathe deeply. "Landon does."

She looks with wide eyes from me and then back to the scribe, her fingers hovering there, and then back to me.

"As in...Jackson?" She's cautious with her question, likely unsure of if I know who he is or not.

I nod quickly and try to remember to breathe. I remember that I didn't tell Sadie about Jackson stopping by Connor's on Tuesday night. It's unlike me to keep a secret so big. I've never kept anything from her, so I'm sure she's confused as to why I'm holding a book from him.

My encounter with him felt strangely...personal, though.

"Jackson as in...Wolf?" She continues.

I nod again.

Her mouth falls open. "Liv."

My brows raise. "Sadie."

"What are you not telling me?"

I sigh, falling back against the futon as I shrug my shoulders. "So, so much. I didn't know if you knew about Landon's... extracurriculars. I didn't want to be a snitch."

She scoffs. "Landon is beside the point right now. The hottest man that I've ever *seen* is sending you *gifts*? With personalized little notes? And I know *nothing* about *anything*?" She crosses her arms and she waits on me to say more, her baby blues full of wonder.

"Sadie! We haven't been talking as much since the game." I defend myself, rightfully.

"Liv, I've apologized. What more can I say or do to make it up to you?"

"It's not that you need to do anything," I say, and reach for the book that's still in her hands. "I just have been preoccupied, I guess. I've been reading this series, and worried about Landon. And working."

She looks at me deadpan. "Well, now I'm here, and now you need to tell me how this came about? You literally don't go out and don't do anything. I don't understand why this—" she leans forward and taps the book a couple times with her pointer finger. "—is in your hands."

"The night before the homecoming game, Landon said I could ride with him to 'take care of something'," I stick my fingers up and air quote, "while my car was being fixed. I didn't know it was to go pay his mob boss for drugs."

"Landon didn't tell you to stay in the car?" She leans closer as if eating up every word I give her.

"Yes, he did. But I guess he said something to Jackson and... things escalated. I had to jump out of the car and try to get Jackson to stop before he killed Landon."

Sadie stares at me with wide eyes and an open mouth for a few moments. I almost laugh until she blinks a few times and shakes her head. "And you are still *alive*? What did you say to him?"

I pull my legs in and cross them, a whisper of a smirk crossing my lips. "I pretty much told him to fuck off."

"You told Jackson Wolf to 'fuck off'?"

I shrug and roll my eyes. "Or some variation of that, yes. Anyways, the next time I saw him…" I trail off, remembering that it was after the game. I never told her about that, either. Her and I haven't talked any more about what happened at the game past her apologizing for it.

"After the game, with the contest…" I bring that image to my mind, my body getting the same surge of wonder when I saw him, then. "I was running to my car and he was there—Jackson was." My eyes find hers. "He was watching the game over the wall by the park, and when I realized he was there, we just…we just stared at each other as he smoked a cigarette, and…I started crying in front of him." Saying it out loud in the open makes me realize that I'm so grateful for the fact that he didn't make fun of me or dwell on it when he saw me at Connor's. He's the only person I've ever let see me cry.

"And then…?"

"And then I literally ran away. Landon visited me the Sunday after and pretty much gave me the run down on what he's into—which, is actually stupid, if you ask me." I tell her, reaching up to twist a strand of hair around my fingers.

Sadie just stares at me with an open mouth. "Liv, we are not worrying about Landon right now, I want to know everything about Mr. Tall, Dark, and Broody."

"There's not much more to tell…I was getting off of work on Tuesday and he was there, waiting for me."

"Waiting for you?" An echo. "For what?"

"He was looking for Landon."

"But Landon doesn't come back from Gatlinburg until tomorrow."

"Right, so why wouldn't he tell his boss about it?" I ask suspiciously.

Sadie shrugs and shakes her head. "It honestly doesn't matter, Liv. What matters is that Jackson Wolf is totally into you, and he's bought you something that he knew you would love. He already knows you better than any guy you've ever been interested in, and isn't shaming you for it."

I blink. "I know, Sadie. But...Landon warned me about him. He almost got his ass kicked by Jackson for telling him to stay away or something. And I know Landon's...feelings for me. I don't want to hurt him."

"Do you feel the same way about Landon?" She asks me.

I shake my head quickly, knowing the answer to that. "No, I don't. It makes me cringe to think of Landon as anything more than a brother. I love him, but like family."

"Exactly. And you have this hot-ass giving you gifts? I'm not a love expert, but, if I were, I would say that this is the beginning of an incredible love story." Sadie smiles widely and nods her head, proud of her hypothesis.

"It's not love, and it won't be in the foreseeable future, Sadie. It's just a book." I say back to her with as much ease as I can muster, and I push myself from the little couch. I toss the book and it lands on the foot of my bed. I promise myself to begin it tonight, I just finished the other one a couple days ago and am impressed with the timing of Jackson's delivery.

But the more that I stand there and look at that book, I know for a fact that it is certainly more than just a book.

At least, for me.

CHAPTER

Six

*W*hen Landon got back into town earlier, he'd sent me a text and asked me to meet him at the weight room at the high school.

Here it is, 4:32 P.M. on Sunday afternoon, and I'm climbing into his truck with my bag draping over my shoulder.

"Hey, Landon, how was the trip?" I ask him as I pull my seatbelt on.

He backs out of his parking spot and blows out a breath. "Well, everyone is alive, and I'm here, but I'm in desperate need of a stress reliever. How was the week without me?" He asks and shoots a wink my way. I smile at him but it starts to fade when I think about Jackson.

"Jackson came to Connor's looking for you. Why didn't you tell him you were going out of town?"

He shrugs and turns the wheel. "It wasn't any of his business."

I pause before continuing. "But shouldn't you tell your boss when you're going to be off work?"

He looks over at me slowly and then back to the road. "What did he do?"

"What do you mean?"

He sighs and rubs his forehead. "Did he hurt you? Force himself on you? When he came to Connor's, what did he do?"

I furrow my brows, remembering Jackson's grip on my chin. It was demanding, yet soft. And left me yearning for more.

My head shakes. "No, nothing like that. He was just wondering where you were." My thoughts almost falter when I think about the book, which I pull from my bag and place on my lap. Once again, I admire its beauty. And for the thousandth time since yesterday, I admire who gifted it to me.

"What did you tell him?" He asks, and turns down that notorious dirt road. I know exactly who we are going to see, and my heart begins to race with anticipation.

I shake my head again, clearing my thoughts of skeleton bone tattoos and green eyes. "Nothing, I figured that if you didn't tell him, then there was a reason. So, I told him I didn't know."

He sighs, running his hand over his face, again. "Thank you for that."

I nod. "It's no problem."

"This is why I didn't want to drag you into this." The tone of Landon's voice is solemn, but before I can ask anything more, he pulls something from his ear and slows his speed down the beaten path. His knee takes the bottom of the wheel and he grabs a lighter, flicking it and setting the end of the…joint?

Is that what that is?

Holy shit.

"Landon, what are you doing? What is that?" I almost feel panicked. This must be the new Landon.

"I told you; I need a stress reliever. You don't have to hit it." And then the cabin fills with the pungent aroma of marijuana.

Oh, my God.

The thick smoke infiltrates my nose and throat and lungs and I almost feel trapped in the cab of his truck.

"I'm not going to get high from this?" I ask him suspiciously.

"In theory, you shouldn't, but maybe you should try it." He grins softly as he blows out a cloud of smoke and he coughs.

No, thank you.

My nose turns up as I look out the window. We arrive at the same intersection, but Jackson isn't there yet.

"I've got a phone call to make, so, I'll crack the windows for you to let this smoke out but I'll step out of the truck to finish smoking. Jackson should be here in a few." Landon tells me as he pushes the truck into park.

I nod my head silently and open the pages of my book, but how could I focus in a moment like this?

My eyes look over the handwritten message in the front of it and I smile, welcoming those butterflies flapping around in my belly.

I try to continue where I left off, only a few pages in, but I can't concentrate. Especially when the low rumble of an engine approaches, and my heart practically stops.

He's here.

I should stay in the truck. Right? Let the men handle what they need to handle. But I don't *want* to do that.

If my heart were to grow feet, it would be halfway to Fanning Springs right now.

Stay where you are, Olivia.

If he wanted to see you, he would. Don't start to get a crush and act like an idiot.

I watch out the window, my hands getting sweaty around the plasticky cover of my book.

Jackson steps out of his car and Landon approaches him, handing him the joint between his fingers. To my surprise,

Jackson takes it and pulls on the end. The window isn't cracked enough to hear what they are saying, but I can tell from the look on Jackson's face that he isn't happy. Even more unhappy than his usual emotionless face.

Just like last time, Landon's back is to me and I can only see Jackson's face as he shuts his driver door and leans against it. He hits the joint a few more times and passes it back to Landon as he listens to whatever is coming out of his mouth, very un-impressed.

Landon finishes the joint and tosses it into the sand. They seem to only be conversing, except in only a moment, everything changes, exactly like it did the very first time I was in this spot.

In one blink, one of Jackson's hands is wrapping around the back of Landon's neck and the other is at the front. My mind spins with the quickness of Jackson's movements, and the sun glinting off the metal gives me the only clue as to what is happening.

Jackson is holding a knife to Landon's throat.

Oh, oh no.

My heart stops and I don't even think before I'm standing next to both of them, my arms out in front of me.

"What in the hell is going on?!" I say to them, but neither of them answer me as I watch the scariest pissing match I've ever seen.

The blood roars in my ears when I see one small dribble of blood run down the edge of the blade from the tip digging into Landon's skin.

"Please! Stop!" I yell, but he only seems to dig the blade deeper into the flesh of Landon's throat.

Landon only glares back at him, nostrils flaring like a mad bull.

He's challenging Jackson.

Landon's crystal blue eyes staring down Jackson's green ones, his intent evident in them.

"You're going to kill him!" I almost screech, only about a foot away from them. Both of them are breathing heavy and I feel like an invisible person when I still get no answer.

Only a thicker and faster stream of blood trickling down that shiny blade. It begins running over Jackson's fingers, coloring those shadowy bones crimson.

What the fuck do I do?

I'll never forgive myself if I stand here and watch my best friend die.

"Jackson," I say calmly, despite the tremble of emotion, and I reach both of my hands out to wrap around that massive forearm. I know that the next thing I'm going to say won't matter to him. He's a murderer. But it's worth a shot. "You're going to *kill him.*"

Jackson finally breaks that hold, those flaming green eyes meeting mine.

My heart skips about three beats, and the pain of that tender muscle faltering captures my breath. I pull my hand away and press a palm against my chest to try to rub the ache out. This isn't fear. No…this is something else entirely.

His eyes drop to my hand against my chest and his features crack for the slightest moment before they return to stone. Jackson pulls away, dropping Landon to the ground. He steps over to his vehicle and snatches a black cloth from his back pocket, cleaning the blade and his hand.

"Once again, your *little* girlfriend saved your *little* balls, Superstar. I'd try treating her with a little more respect than you have been." I don't think that he could sound any more disgusted than he does right now. I decide to completely overlook his exaggeration of the word *little.*

I force myself to pull my eyes from the more-than-human image before me and drop to the ground, next to my injured best friend.

A strange sense of dejavu covers me as I grip Landon's jaw and turn his head to inspect the cut. Red stains his neck and shirt, but the cut is superficial.

"The next time you don't report, and you fucking lie to me about your whereabouts," Jackson says, as deep as death, "I don't care if she's here or not. I will cut you open from ear to ear." And he looks back to us on the ground as he tucks his blade away.

"You learn your place, or you'll be removed from the game." He adds before he opens his door. Jackson's eyes fall to my chest and the strangest look crosses his features before he slowly trails up my neck, then to my lips, and up to my eyes.

"Remember what I told you, Olivia. Demand the respect that you deserve." His voice covers me like a blanket and I almost shiver in the warm autumn afternoon.

Landon coughs next to me and I rub his back softly, providing some sort of comfort, but Jackson speaks again.

"Oh, and Olivia?" My head whips back to him. "I do hope you enjoy that book. It was exponentially better than the first two, in my opinion."

I swallow the cough threatening to burst out, and before I even begin to think about the many feelings that erupt from the dimpled smile he flashes me, I put them in a box, shelve the box, and turn my sights back to my best friend.

The echo of a dark chuckle is the only thing that I remember hearing before the low rumble of his engine fading away, and I'm left with his mess.

I figured going back to my house was the best idea since Landon's dad and stepmom are...insane. We can sneak past Nana and get him cleaned up before he goes home. I think I have a shirt or two of his stuffed in one of my drawers from the nights he's stayed over.

It's only about six in the evening when we pull down the lane to my home, but the time is about to change, and it gets dark early. This aids us for obvious reasons. Landon kills the headlights as we pull up to the house.

He sits outside the door, and waits on my text that he can come in.

Much to my surprise, Nana has already made dinner, cleaned up, and put the leftovers in Tupperware for me to make a plate when I got home.

I could smell it when I walked inside. Chicken and dumplings. My stomach rumbles despite the events that happened only an hour before.

"When we get you cleaned up, I'll make you a plate." I say to Landon as we cross the kitchen and head up the stairs to my room.

We take our spot in the bathroom, Landon sitting on the counter and me standing between his knees as I clean the blood off his skin with a warm and wet cloth.

"What did you say to him to piss him off?"

Landon's unfocused blue eyes find mine and he swallows, his throat rolling underneath my touch.

"I told him to leave you the fuck alone, that you're mine." His voice is gruff and I clear my throat, continuing to clean his skin.

"Shirt." I tell him and back up for him to lift his shirt over his head. Luckily not much blood went through his shirt, only a few streaks, so I wipe them quickly, careful not to dwell on how this might seem with us standing so close.

I turn to the sink and rinse the rag, red streaming the bowl.

"Landon, you know that I'm no—"

"I know, Olivia." Landon stops my words and I clamp my mouth shut. "I just don't want this fuck-head to think that he has a chance with you. You're..." He looks down, looking for the words. "You're too good."

"Too good?"

He nods, and I push his chin up so I can apply a butterfly bandage. "Too good for him. For me. For anyone in this shit town."

My fingers work quickly and I turn to leave the tense air, entering my room once more. I tug on a drawer and rummage, searching for the biggest t-shirt I can find.

At one point of my life, I would have rejoiced at hearing those words, knowing in my soul that I wasn't good enough for anyone in Chiefland. It goes right along with the fact that I'm leaving.

Except...I feel like I finally met someone that knows me, and the words that Landon just laid on me leaves me feeling... dread.

"Here's a shirt for you," I say into the air and then toss it to him as he emerges from the bathroom. "I'll go make you a plate."

I leave him to get dressed as I walk out of my room, down to the kitchen, and make two heaping plates of chicken and dumplings.

We share a silent supper in my room. Landon seems lost in his thoughts, and I can't stop looking at the bandage that covers the skin on his neck. My mind still replaying the actions that took place.

Just how natural it was for Jackson to pull that knife.

Just how that blood ran down his arm.

I set my futon up for him to sleep, tossing some extra pillows and blankets on there for Landon. He thanks me quietly and lays down as I excuse myself to the bathroom and shut the door behind me.

When I turn to look in the mirror, a gasp escapes me.

A bold and crimson handprint rests on my white t-shirt.

My brows pull in confusion as I reach up and place my hand directly over it, and I think back to when I grabbed Jackson's arm. The blood must have been running down his arm and covered my hand.

That's what Jackson was looking at before he left.

Chills run over my skin and I rid my clothes, taking a quick shower before getting ready for my bed.

Before I even settle into my bed, I can hear Landon's soft snores and I'm grateful for the time alone.

I didn't shut my curtain when we got home, and I can see the full moon high in the sky as I lay my head on my pillow.

Again, I find my thoughts drifting back to how Jackson looked with that blade. It was so easy for him, so natural to draw Landon's blood. It should have terrified me, sent me running for the hills.

But it's done the complete opposite.

Jackson's words infiltrate my mind. *"I do hope you enjoy that book. It was exponentially better than the first two, in my opinion."*

Does that mean that he already read the first two? And the third? That would mean that he read…1,900 pages in five days? Can people even read that fast?

If he did…the thought sends a legion of butterflies through my belly. Nobody I've ever known has been interested in me enough to know what I'm reading, let alone read it themselves.

I'm grateful that Landon didn't ask about the book when Jackson brought it up. Landon's being incredibly defensive over me, but...I'm not his to claim. I'm not anyone's to claim.

I'm glad that Landon is safe and sleeping peacefully on my futon, but I do wonder what would have happened if I weren't there. Would he be dead? Landon didn't tell Jackson where he was going, and I don't know why.

As much as I don't want to, I wonder what Jackson is doing. Is he laying in his bed thinking about...me? It seems silly to think about Jackson doing something like *sleeping*.

As if he's some immortal being and doesn't rest.

Finally, after about an hour of tossing and turning, my mind drifts into that sleepy void, and I'm met with vivid green eyes emerging from the darkness, and strangely dreaming of those gorgeous lips on my skin.

CHAPTER

Seven

"*Y'all need to leave, my daughter is sleeping!*" *My mother's urgent voice startled me awake. I sat straight up when a couple of bumps and screeches followed.*

A dark and disgusting set of laughs rumble down the hallway like monsters in the dark. "Well, you better hope she sleeps hard."

In my eleven-year-old mind, my mother was in trouble, and I needed to help. I would help, no matter what I had to do.

My bare feet carried me down the hallway and into the kitchen, as fast as they would go.

My mother was on the pale yellow carpet in the living room, kicking her legs and thrashing her arms. I halted right where I was in the threshold when her eyes met mine and she shook her head.

Allison Hayes was never a good mother. She never wanted me, and was never shy about vocalizing the fact. I don't remember one time where I was happy that I was my mother's daughter.

Except, this one split moment, where she warned me not to come any closer. This one time in my life, I knew I needed to listen to her.

There were four men, all average looking and of average build. I couldn't pick them out of a line up. They were all dressed in dark jeans and dark coats, and I remember thinking that was very strange considering how hot it always is in Florida.

The men began to close in on her, and I heeded her silent warning and began to back away, however, a giant hand clamping down on my shoulder stopped me.

"And where do you think you're going? The party was just starting! Let's go join them," A hot gruff voice hit the back of my neck and my ear, and a stroke of ice froze my insides.

No, no, no. This isn't happening.

The man pushes me further into the room and I step away from him, attempting to run for the door. Maybe I can get far enough away and get her help.

But, one of the other men steps in front of the doorway with a disgusting grin, his jowls jiggling as he walks.

"Oh, no, Princess. We are going to watch." The first man that found me in the hallway says from the other side of the room, and I look to my mother, desperate.

Desperate for escape.

Desperate for something to do.

Desperate to wake up from this nightmare.

But, when I find her eyes again, they are distant. She's gone somewhere else, leaving me here to experience whatever this is going to be all alone.

A hot hand grips my wrist, tugs me across the living room, and plops me on the chair.

The man sits with me, next to me, and begins speaking as the others close in on my mother, who is no longer fighting. The fear that grips my entire being pushes me into sort of the same state. I sit there, like a good little girl, and I do what I'm told.

"Your mommy was a very bad girl, and she is going to be punished for it. This is a life lesson, Princess. I'm sorry you have to experience it this way, but we all have to grow up some time."

My body jolts awake, sitting straight up in bed with my hands bracing me. There's not enough air in the room to fill my lungs.

Sweat coats my neck, and back, and half of my hair is wet from it.

"Oh, God…" I whisper to myself, my fingers rubbing the images away from my eyes. It's been a long time since I've had that dream. A couple years, at least.

I pull myself from bed and wrap my long hair up in a bun with an elastic, letting the cool air dry my neck and back. My feet carry me down the stairs and to the kitchen, filling a glass of water from the tap, and carrying it out to the back porch.

Fresh air fills my lungs and my mind instantly feels clearer. I'm not sure what time it is, but the sky is still deep blue with flecks of starlight and I know it's nowhere near morning when the crickets sound off as I settle into my rocking chair.

That night, I felt completely and utterly helpless. I was disgusted. I felt sick. I wanted to scream and cry and run away to anywhere but there.

My mother was violated in any and every way imaginable, and I was made to watch. Every time I tried to close my eyes or look away, that man was there to redirect me.

Before then, I'd known what sex was. Every kid knows by the age of seven or eight when you have a public-school education. But what I witnessed that night was something else entirely. It changed something inside me. I vowed to never, ever, get involved with any man. To never put myself in a position where I feel that helpless again.

I decided in that moment that love wasn't real. Love was something that was made up and only in fairy tells and books and movies. How could it be real when I saw what happened to my mother? What happened that night was pure evil, and what happened after rivaled it.

The cool water hits my throat and my mind takes me back through that tragedy.

When the men left, I helped my mother limp to the shower, my eleven-year-old frame trying to support her as best as possible. Even at eleven, I was already bigger than every other person in my grade—even the boys—so I felt aptly qualified for the job.

I peeled the scraps of clothes off of her and I helped her into the shower, washing her hair and washing her body as carefully as I could.

She was silent the entire time, still lost in that faraway land she retreated to. I wished desperately that I could do more—to say something that might bring her back, but I knew it was a fruitless attempt. She'd gone into a state like this before, and nothing I did or said could pull her back.

It wasn't until I got her into her bed that she came back to me, and when she did, her only words to me before turning over and falling asleep were, "If you'd tried *harder*, none of this would have happened."

Even as a child, I knew that what happened to my mother wasn't my fault. I was a victim as much as she, but knowing that in my heart didn't make it hurt less when she delivered that verbal punch to my gut.

Since then, I try as hard as I can in everything I do. She is the reason that I refuse to stay in this town. I will try as hard as I can to make something of myself, someone that even Allison Hayes would be proud of.

If she were here.

That sad little girl inside is a little bummed sometimes that my mother hasn't seen me go through high school. I doubt she will see me graduate. Maybe it's for the best though.

After that rare trip down memory lane, my mind feels... clouded, that overwhelming warmth heating my neck and ears.

I know that I won't be able to find sleep again after that nightmare. I never can. So, I finish the rest of my water and I make my way back upstairs to my room. I pull a black hoodie and yank a pair of pink sweatpants up my legs.

And before I know it, I'm behind the wheel, beginning the ten-minute drive into town.

CHAPTER

Eight

Chiefland, Florida is a ghost town at night. Everyone is tucked away safely in their beds and the only action that you might see is the occasional semi-truck passing through or resting at the Circle K.

If you are watching closely and paying attention, you can almost see the tweakers and the fugitives walking along the shadows and the tree line.

No offense to the town that I love and grew up in, but it's a fact. It's a growing issue. Too many drugs and too many sad and lonely people. It's the perfect equation.

Also, Chiefland's small population makes it easy for more people to be running from the law.

Child support.

Failure to appear.

Traffic ticket.

So many mundane things to be running from jail for, when all you had to do was pay your fine or show up in front of the judge.

They are misunderstood, though. Sometimes life just doesn't work out the way you want it to even though it's the easy thing to do.

And then they are stuck. Confined to moving in the night and in the shadows during the day.

My little car struggles to change gears as I come into the town, slowing to a stop at the last stop light in Chiefland on South Side. I decided that I needed ice cream to go back to sleep, even though it's 3:17 in the morning.

I'll go to Walmart. It's the only 24-hour store in Chiefland.

The cool autumn breeze tickles my cheeks and my warm neck as I roll the windows down. With the speed limit only 35 MPH through down town, it doesn't blow my hair around too much and I can leisurely ride through town without worrying about people looking at me...or me, them.

I love the serenity of the early morning, the peacefulness, and the only real quiet that I can find. When the only ones awake are the ones that don't want to be found.

I turn left, past Gasmart on the intersection to the left, and began heading North on US 19. The dull yellow night lamps are the only light that's provided. Clear skies were over my house but here in town is a different story. I can smell the rain that will soon drop as the breeze carries it through the cab of my car.

Walmart is on the North side of town, so I must go through every single stop light through town. I pass a slew of old, abandoned buildings on both sides of the four-lane road that were once thriving businesses. A red light catches me at the first intersection after I turned, stopping me in front of Chiefland Police Department, but it's a dark building. No lights, no sign of life. Chiefland has police and a police department, but the city police doesn't have any holding cells. Only Levy County Sheriff's Office, so Levy County Jail in Bronson is the only city in Levy to actually have a jail. Only a few patrol cars on duty at all times in Chiefland.

Lucky for the night-walkers.

A green light signals for me to go after only a few seconds. I pass the Government Aid building on my right, and on my left, an old strip with a consignment shop, a thrift store, and a plumbing supply store. On my right is a couple more abandoned buildings and an antique store. On my left is a bigger strip with a restaurant, a nail salon, a 24-hour gym, a few more thrift stores, the probation office, and the tax collector. On the right, the building on the intersection is a hair salon and a realty building in one.

Every single building up to that intersection is completely dark. I can barely even see the palm trees tucked between each building; I certainly can't see whatever lurks in those shadows.

This one is a green light, and I go right through, passing the strip to my right, including a gas station, a hair salon, and a flower shop, and the strip of doctor's offices to my left.

Despite the cool breeze whipping softly around my head and through the cab, my hands begin to sweat against the steering wheel.

I haven't passed one vehicle, and that almost unnerves me. Maybe it's just my nerves after my waking up from that nightmare.

And, just went I start to believe myself that it's all in my head, a shadow flits across the tree-line to my left, and I yank my sights to try to catch a glimpse.

Bang!

The sound of flesh and bone colliding with the hard plastic of my vehicle's bumper forces me to stomp on the break before I even whip my head forward. The quickest flash of a tan-colored hide is in my vision before it's off to the side of my car, just out of the headlights.

A deer. A fucking deer.

"Oh, my God!" I cry to myself, emotion beginning to bubble in my chest. I've never hit an animal before, and although I'm not the praying type, I'm praying hard that I didn't just slaughter one.

My hand throws my car into park in the middle of the road, and I press my flashers, sending a blinking yellow across the left lane and median.

The deer gets its shaky legs up under her and falls again, attempt once more to regain her balance. Guilt and anger flood my chest as I watch it struggle just outside of my car.

What do I do?

I carefully pull the door handle with trembling fingers, popping open the door. The deer jumps at the sudden noise and tries to escape again, but its entire back half is limp against the ground now, unable to move any further.

That damn muscle twists behind my ribcage.

Besides my pulse, the only sounds are my car's idling engine, the swishing of the palms in the soft breeze overhead, a low rumble of thunder in the distance, and the clacking of the deer's hooves against the pavement, desperately trying to make an escape.

She manages to pull herself a few more feet but she's still in the middle of the left lane, trying to get across the median and to the other side.

So, I do the only sensible thing I can think of.

I hold my hands out in front of me as I step in front of her, the light of my flashers reflecting off of her tan coat. Her black eyes follow me as I round her and I reach down to touch the soft hide on her long neck.

"Shhh, girl, you're going to be okay," I whisper to her. "I'm so sorry. So, so, sorry."

All logic in my mind tells me that she will not, in fact, be okay. She could never fend for herself now. She will die, and that thought...

"I'm going to get you across the road, girl." I say a bit stronger, and then I reach down and hook my hands underneath her front legs, right in the pits.

She breathes heavy, hot air pushing out of her black nose, but she doesn't object. I use all my strength to pull as hard as I can. I'm able to drag her a couple of inches with several grunts and groans.

I look behind me and we are only about six feet away from the median, and then two more entire lanes. My shoulder's slump with the slightest bit of defeat, but I shake my head and gather my wits.

"Don't beat yourself before you've even given it a shot." I encourage myself   and resume my position, tugging and tugging and tugging and tugging.

The doe attempts to help me and get her back legs up under her, but it's to no avail.

My heart thunders like the storm brewing overhead as I heave as hard as I can, using every muscle available to get this poor animal across the road. I pay no mind to any other thing except this.

I owe her the decency of getting her across the road. Especially when I just signed her death sentence.

I tug one more time, hoping that I only need a couple more, and then before I know what's happening, my feet are off the ground and I'm in the air, whirling around.

Alarm bells sound in my head as my eyesight shifts from the deer still on the asphalt to the night sky above and then the grass of the median underneath me. I realize that an arm is around my waist, pulling me away from the animal and I begin to kick my legs in objection.

"No! No! I have to help her! Put me down!" I scream, tears and emotion welling up in my throat and chest.

Before I can break free and get my feet under me, the deafening roar of an engine floods my ears and blinding headlights blur my vision. The grill of a Mack truck is the last thing I see before the reflection of the headlights glinting off the deer's black eyes.

I don't even hear myself scream as I whirl around to avoid seeing the horrific accident. My face collides with a body, and I can feel their hands on my back, rubbing in comfortable strokes and pulling me further into their chest.

Unable to stop it, a sob rocks through me, and I cling to the stability of a stranger, as the burn of helplessness and guilt settles into my stomach, like a bag of rocks.

The semi's engine fades away as it continues on North through town and my tears cease when I recognize the unmistakable and overwhelming scent of cigarettes...coffee... and leather.

I push away from the embrace and don't try to hide the disgust on my face. Jackson's hair is especially unruly, dark locks tumbling over his forehead. His wild, animalistic eyes burn just as bright as they do in the day time.

Fucking gorgeous even in the shadows of the night. His distracting beauty is absolutely fucking *maddening*, especially after he just stopped me from helping an animal that *I* injured.

"What were you thinking, Olivia?" He asks, his tone smooth and calm.

My chest heaves up and down as I take a few deep and shaky breaths, admiring his audacity.

"I was getting her across the street, Jackson! I h—" My voice falters, choked by a cry, and I clear my throat to begin again. "I h-hit her. She needed help."

His brow furrows. "It's a deer. They die all the time."

I scoff with tears in my eyes, appalled by his insensitivity. "Every life matters." I can feel the tremble in my voice as my emotion threatens to break free.

"Every life may matter, Olivia, but not every life needs to be saved."

A burst of air expels from my lungs. "Yeah, you wouldn't know anything about saving lives, would you? Mr. Death and fucking Destruction!" Hot, angry tears slip down my cheeks.

"I just saved your life, didn't I?!"

"I didn't ask you to!" I scream, taking a few steps backwards away from him.

"Oh, trust me," a dark, deep, disgusted voice stands the hair on my neck up. "I didn't fucking want to."

Ouch.

My jaw clenches, a failed attempt at stopping his words from slicing too deep, but oh, *my god*, that hurt.

Jackson turns his back to me and lifts his hands to wipe his face. My blood roars in my ears.

"It would have been so much easier to let that truck smear you from here to Fanning. This fucking turmoil would have been no more. You've complicated my life by simply existing and here you go creating more problems by putting yourself in harm's way. You are *so infuriating*, Olivia," he turns back to me, then steps toward me with his eyes ablaze, "do you not have just one notion of self-preservation!?"

I shrug my shoulders in response, the tears falling freely now. Not caring that I'm quite literally wearing my emotion.

"I guess I don't, Jackson Wolf. Not that it matters to you. I've heard all about the horrible person you are and the unthinkable things you do." I let it gush out, not missing the flinch that crinkles his expression. As if *I* could hurt *his* feelings.

"You know," he begins, his tone as soft as butter. "I didn't think that a girl as smart as you would so easily blur the line between bravery and stupidity."

"Stupidity?!"

He steps toward me but I only lift my chin to look in his eyes, not daring to back down despite the wetness on my cheeks and in my eyes.

"Yes, stupid! Dumb! Idiotic! Fucking moronic! What you just did is absolutely *stupid*! You could have died! Just like the first time we met, and the time after that. If you were anyone else," he breathes out, his voice now above a whisper, but it still licks along my neck, "I would have taken your life for getting involved with something that had *nothing to do with you*."

Our noses and lips only a couple inches apart. The acid in his eyes churns when they drop to my mouth to watch me speak. "Maybe you should have." I challenge, my words breaking. His nostrils flare in response and something passes in his eyes. Something that I want to personify, but tears his gaze from mine and turns away. A cool, storm-laden breeze fills his spot.

Jackson takes a few steps and stops, turning his head slightly, but doesn't meet my eye. Of course, he would deny be that satisfaction of seeing his face one last time. "From now on, it would be smart of you to stay away from the group of friends you have. You don't belong in this life. You should get out of it before it kills you."

The darkness whispers with the swishing of the pines and palm trees, welcoming Jackson's presence and swallowing him whole.

I stand there, watching him become part of those shadows like he's an apparition rather than a man.

I stand there, shaking with emotion. Every emotion imaginable.

I stand there, the guilt of taking a life weighing heavy on my chest.

And he leaves me there, underneath the stormy night sky, in the grassy median, with a dead deer on the road and my flashing lights keeping me company.

CHAPTER

Nine

*F*or the first time in my life, I listened to a man when he told me that I needed to do something.

He had a completely valid point, simply asking me to stay away from the group of friends that could, and would, if I were to let them, lead me down the wrong path.

In retrospect, if I were to take a step back and look at my situation from a sane person's point of view; if I wanted to continue on my path that I'm currently set on and have every intention of going down, I *should* sever ties between my friends and me, given the life choices that they've both made recently. Guilty by association, is what they say, and the last thing that I want to do is ruin my life simply for being there with them. Aren't most inmates wrongfully prosecuted? Wrong place, wrong time? It's the smart and logical thing to do. To keep on my course. To be the woman that I want to be.

That night I went home and I took the longest shower I've ever taken and I cried for hours. I cried for the deer's life that was lost. I cried for myself, and losing that animal because I wasn't paying attention to what I was doing. I cried for the way that I believed those hateful words that Jackson had said, telling me I was dumb and idiotic for trying to save the deer. It made me feel like the child that tried to save her mother from getting hurt. His words watered that seed of hopelessness that I thought had withered up and dried out.

I cried because the way that he left felt a lot like "goodbye," and I was just beginning to want to say "hello." While his words burned my ego, I felt hope when I looked at him. And the moment he walked away, I found myself wanting to tell him to come back.

I'd barely known him, and I mourned losing him...and that's kind of crazy. So, I knew that I *needed* to separate from my friends and refocus on *me*.

I've done the best I can at staying away from Sadie and Landon. For an entire month.

The only time that I've actually hung out with either of them is when they come to my house and see me, which hasn't been a lot. I've texted Sadie and invited her over to my house more times than she's already been over, but she's been running around with Ryan and "busy".

Landon...

My heart hurts for Landon. Whispers in the hallways tell me that he officially dropped out last week.

No more football.

No more full-ride scholarship.

No more future that he worked so hard for.

He's 100% committed to the life that he's living.

I only hope that it has the outcome that he's intending with his mother's sickness. I hope more than anything that he makes it out alive. Last week, I saw him walking across the street from the school and on his skin, he wore the same tattoo that Jackson does.

Those shadowy bones over his hands and arms.

I wonder what he did to finally get them.

My mind reaches into the gutter and I can only think the absolute worst. The fact is that the Landon he's become is somebody entirely different than the one that I grew up with and love, and my heart can't hurt for him.

Not anymore.

We are old enough now that we are making our own paths and he's made his choice. And so, it's been a month since I saw a glimpse of the pain that I could go through if it gets too far and goes south.

Today is Halloween. Whenever it falls on a weekday, I typically stay home from school and work. Surprises and masks and dressing up isn't really my thing. On October 30th, I normally stock up on candy, and on the 31st, I binge watch *Supernatural* until I fall asleep.

I do that every single year, with the exception for this year. This year, it falls on a Wednesday, and Sadie has invited me to a party that's taking place out on the back part of Old Man Taylor's property. She said something about a car meet, or a bonfire.

I did skip school, and also stocked up on candy, though, and I'll be taking it with me to munch on when I get bored like I always do at parties.

This is probably why I'm "big-boned" as I've been described by several of the boys in our grade.

Every light in Sadie's house is on when I arrive for us to get ready, and I make my way through the fake spider webs at the front door to get inside.

"Oh, Olivia! It's so good to see you, sweetie. How have you been?" Sadie's mother, Marcia, greets me as soon as I get in. Her wide smile is full of life and her baby blue eyes remind me of Sadie's. Both of them share a face, and Sadie's father, Harold, looks like a caveman with his brown hair braided down his back. He shoots me wave and a smile when he enters the room.

"I've been good, Ms. Marcia. Sadie's in her room?" I offer a wave and I stand awkwardly at the front door as she dumps bags of candy in the massive bowl. She nods and turns to kiss her husband in "true-love" fashion.

I step away, making my way down the hallway to Sadie's room at the very end.

A strange feeling resonates with me after seeing Marcia and Harold's kiss. I hope one day that I get to experience that kind of love.

"Sadie?" I call out and push the door open to her room. She has the windows open and she is rummaging through her closet.

"In here!" She calls out from behind a pile of clothes. I'm a little shocked by the unmistakable smell of marijuana.

I clear my throat and take a look around without her, noticing the small tray with green buds, a lighter, a foil package, and an ash tray sitting on her nightstand.

Suddenly, I feel like I'm standing in a stranger's room. I didn't realize that Sadie had gotten into weed so much.

She stumbles out of her closet with several items of clothes draping over her forearm.

"Happy Halloween!" She exclaims and grins at me. "We are going to have so much fun tonight!"

I doubt it.

"Happy Halloween, Sade." I respond with a smile as I shed my hoodie and drop my bag by the door, and sit down on the end of her bed.

"So, I've got this here," she says, laying out the clothes on her bed. "I figured you could wear this one. It's a little large for m—"

"I'm perfectly fine wearing what I have on, Sadie." I interject as soft as I can, trying not to hurt her feelings.

She eyes me closely and a mischievous grin erupts on her perfect face, but she doesn't comment. Instead, she sets all the clothes down and walks around to the front of her bed, plopping down. She reaches for the small tray on her nightstand and I take a deep breath but don't say anything. It's her house, if her parents don't care that she's doing it, then I don't either.

"I haven't seen you much, Liv." She says as she begins breaking the green bud on the tray into small...crumbs? "How have you been?"

I shake my head, ready to tell her that I've been good, just doing my same old same old. But I stop myself.

"I've been lonely." I say, the truth of my words surprising me.

Her eyes meet mine for a moment and then she looks back down to her lap, pulling a long brown cigarillo from the foiled pouch.

And I have been. I normally have Sadie and Landon, but I've barely seen them, and I'm longing for some kind of socialization.

"Landon has been out of town, pretty much. He's been working." She says as she splits the cigar down the middle, dumping the junk inside of it into the ashtray.

I nod. "I saw that he got that...tattoo."

She grins. "It's pretty hot, isn't it?"

My mind flashes with an image of Jackson's tattoo, on Jackson's arms and hands, and the several times I've seen them, and touched them, and—

"Oookay, Olivia, you can stop mind-fucking whoever you're thinking about over there!" Her giggle pulls my attention to her and I shake my head as my cheeks flush. I try my hardest to hide my smile but it doesn't work, it never has with Sadie.

"Is it Jackson?" She queries, but my mouth hangs open like a fish out of water. She stays silent, waiting for me to continue, as she sprinkles the broken bud into the empty cigar.

All I can do is shake my head and deny. "It's nobody, Sadie, truly."

Because it's really not.

Not anymore.

Not ever again.

"I know we haven't been hanging out a lot, but I'll try not to be offended over the fact that you think I don't know you." She grins at me and begins licking the brown paper, sealing it shut.

I smirk at her. "You pretend not to be offended, and I'll pretend that you're not rolling a blunt in front of me." I gesture towards her lap.

Sadie and I used to walk to her house every day after school. In middle school and the first two years of high school, we'd have to exit out of the back of the property, by the Ag Building. Our route passed the skatepark and we would always whisper and giggle about the kids in a huddle with smoke coming out of the top of their group.

I never thought we'd be sitting here like this.

She raises the blunt to her lips, sealing it the rest of the way, and flicks the lighter, setting it ablaze.

"Pretend that I'm not smoking it, too." She grins.

The smoke billows around her and into the space above, and it hits me like a brick wall.

"When do we have to leave?" I ask her, trying to change the subject, but not prude enough to move out of the way. I'll be a big girl and inhale whatever comes my way. Even if I think it's fucking disgusting.

She shrugs, blowing out a puff of thick smoke. "It doesn't matter. Party starts at nine."

I nod in response, watching her watch me, and my reaction to her smoking.

"You should really try this, Liv. I think it would take your edge off a ton." She giggles. She must already be high.

A snort flies from my nose. "I don't have an edge."

She throws her head back. "Ha!" She looks at me again and rolls the blunt between her fingers. "You've had the biggest fucking edge since you found out about Landon and Jackson. Like somebody stuck a pole up your ass and hasn't bothered taking it out." She pulls on the end of the blunt again, inhaling.

I swallow my annoyance. Because, it absolutely feels like that.

"I'm just worried for my friend." I tell her, finding a random loose thread on her comforter—which, I realize that her bed isn't made. The Sadie that I knew, that I was friends with, would never ever let the day go without making her bed.

She truly is a different person. I bet it's because of that devil's lettuce she's burning between us. She's lost her drive and her ambition.

When did this happen? When did my best friend change?

I try not to dwell on it though, because if I were to step out of my body and look at us, I probably have my nose turned up like a stuck-up-bitch. And...that's not how I want to treat my best friend.

"So, what kind of party is this tonight? Only people from school will be there, right?" My question is valid.

I've made a valiant attempt to stay away from riff-raff, and if Jackson or Landon is going to be there...

"Right. I don't think anyone else will be. It's supposed to be, like, a race between the triplets and Dalton and Kyle? I know there will be a bonfire. A couple of the girls, maybe." She says purposefully, and then looks over my clothes. "Please, *please* at least wear one of my shirts. Keep the jeans! Whatever! But please dress up, just a little!"

Her pitiful begging has me cracking a smile and I finally give in "Okay, okay. Fine! Fine. Whatever."

For a few moments, it feels like normal again. Our playful banter and shit-talking throws me back only a year's time. About a half of her blunt has burned down, and I'm not sure if I'm anxious about seeing people outside of school for the first time in a while, or if my stomach is nervous from being in a room filled with weed smoke, but I'm eyeing the remainder of the digit between her fingers.

"I started smoking a couple months ago. I lost my scholarship, and I knew you wouldn't approve." For the first time in a while, I hear that small voice of Sadie's and I blink a few times, registering her words.

"You lost your scholarship?"

She nods, pulling on the end of the blunt again and unfolding her legs to push them out in front of her.

"There's so much that I haven't told you, Liv. I'm sorry for keeping you in the dark. It's not like us to keep things from each other." She says, pushing down whatever meek wall I'd built in the month I've barely seen her.

With her apology, my shoulders relax and I pull myself further into her bed, leaning against the wall that it's pushed up against.

"I lost a baby, too." Her voice is…sad. And edgy. Disassociated, almost.

My eyes widen as wide as they can go. My best friend lost a baby and I had no idea?

"W—Wh…" I try to form words but I don't even know the right questions to ask. I'm stunned into silence.

Who's is it? What happened? Why didn't you tell me? *Are you okay?*

I decide to go with the sensible option and everything else will follow.

"Are you okay?"

She smiles softly and inhales once more, nodding. "I'm better now. Ryan's helped me through it. And sweet, sweet Mary Jane."

So, it was Ryan's baby?

She holds the blunt up and grins, her eyes falling lower the more she smokes. She's definitely more relaxed than when I walked in.

I take the wordless moment to account my own relaxed state, even though I haven't smoked it myself.

But what would happen if I did? Marijuana isn't even considered a drug in most states. Trying it won't make me an addict.

I eye the small piece of blunt as she ashes it next to her on the nightstand and raises a blonde brow.

"Wanna try?"

I begin to object by shaking my head, but it stops at a tilt and I reconsider.

Do I?

"What will it do?" I inquire with squinted eyes.

"Well…" She says, repositioning herself to hand it to me. I take it and inspect it, noticing how I can feel the warmth permeating off of the end. "It will make you happy, hungry, and sleepy." She giggles.

Surely, I have enough willpower to not become a crack-head. Going to LA, I'm going to be on the straight and narrow. I deserve to have this one experience where I can tell my children one day that—yes, I tried the weed.

So...I do.

I lift it to my lips and Sadie watches me with excitement. "Do I just...?"

"Just pull it into your mouth like you're sucking from a straw, and inhale what's in your mouth." She directs.

So...I do.

The smoke is thick, and as soon as it hits my throat, I cough it back out, causing Sadie to giggle.

"I did the same thing my first time, go ahead, try again."

So...I do.

I try a couple more times as Sadie tells me about her secret pregnancy that didn't last for long, and how it ended. She still omits the father, and that makes me suspicious, but she continues to just jabber away. About school, how she's failing, and that's what caused her to lose her scholarship. I hold the blunt, and continue to take the smallest hits of it, and she keeps on talking, now about random shit.

I'm assuming to keep me distracted. I hand the blunt back to her, and she to me, and we do that until the entire thing is finished and she's dropping the small piece that's left into the ashtray.

And I feel...strangely...elevated?

My face slightly tingles and my skin is warm, but I'm comfortable.

I thought I would feel like I did drugs, but I just feel... relaxed. And happy. My eyelids hang low, just like Sadie's, and I can still smell the marijuana in the room even though it's not burning anymore.

"Your parents don't mind you smoking?" I ask her.

She shakes her head. "My dad buys it for me. He knows I've been going through a hard time."

Dad of the year.

"I'm sorry I haven't been there." I say, and she shakes her head again.

"I'm sorry I haven't *let* you be there. I'm ashamed of my life. I turned into the person that we vowed never to be when we were younger, and I guess…" Her eyes go distant. "I didn't want to share that with you."

My heart hurts for my best friend. She's been there for me more times than I can count, and really hasn't ever let me down. The football game was a one-time thing. We've already been over that. I've probably been the shit friend most times, and I definitely have been by not being available enough to know about her pregnancy.

"Well, it's a good thing that I'm in the same boat that you are now, so, I have no room to judge, *at all.*" I gesture to my relaxed state and grin at her.

We burst out into laughter together, and I realize that I really have missed her.

"So," I begin, looking over at the articles of clothing. I lean over and take one between my fingers, thumbing the fabric. "Show me what you were gonna put me in."

Sadie's warm smile stretches and we both jump up out of bed, and begin getting ready for our Halloween night.

CHAPTER

Ten

Old Man Taylor is the biggest property owner in Chiefland. I think somebody told me once that he owns over half the town, including the land that the Police Department and City Hall is on. The one we are going to is in Turkey Town, about a mile and a half outside Chiefland's city limits, heading towards Bronson.

It's mainly just fields. Cow and horse pastures. Acres and acres and acres of grass and trees and dirt roads.

We are following behind somebody, the set of red lights coating the interior of my car. Sadie is driving, of course.

I took about five hits too many.

The field is wide open, shielded by miles of woods on all sides, with the exception of a dirt road cut right down the middle of it. To the left, cars and trucks line up along the tree line, about three or four rows already.

The entrance is decorated with fake skeletons and jack-o-lanterns and spider webs hanging from the trees.

In the middle of the field on the right side of the dirt road is a massive bonfire, probably burning five or six feet tall and just as wide. Everybody around it has chairs that they are sitting in, or mingling by the tables set up not far from the fire. Sadie explained that Annmarie Booker's mother provided all the food.

Brooke Halifax's big brother bought all the booze. And as we park and walk up to the table of food and drinks, sure enough, there's an entire table of bottles and cans. Cases of beer are stacked under the table along with more, unopened bottles of liquor and wine.

The food and drink tables are decorated as well. Giant black cauldrons sit in the middle of each of them, a smoky substance pouring out of the top—dry ice most likely. Bowls of candy and candy corn sit in random spots for people to take at their leisure.

Sadie guides me through the growing crowd, me like a shadow behind her. The wind blows softly and it's surprisingly cool, especially on my exposed mid-section.

I agreed to wear what Sadie picked out—a shirt to match my jeans—since I'm living on the wild side tonight already. The sleeves are sheer, thin, and like a second skin, and the solid part of the shirt cuts off right above my belly button. With Sadie being a few sizes smaller, it accentuates my definitely-already-there boobs that jiggle with every step. I can already feel the stares of every person I walk past.

Even with what I'm wearing, though, I still feel out of place. Everybody is dressed up in a costume or their faces painted in some way. Sadie wears a cute little green dress and little fairy wings off of her back. She pasted crystals onto her cheeks and has a color-changing lipstick on. Her hair is balled up on both sides of her head in little space buns.

"Here, try this!" Sadie smiles at me and shoves an orange solo cup in my hands. We are moving down the drink table, but I'm eyeing the food. The grumble in my stomach reminds me of something.

I'm starving.

I take a sip of the cool liquid and am pleasantly surprised. It doesn't taste all that bad.

"What is it?" I ask her. She starts to pour a brown liquid into two other cups.

"White Zinfandel. I figured we should start you out small." She grins at me. "But I want you to take a shot with me first." She takes both cups from the table, hands me one, and nods her head excitedly as I bring it to my lips.

The smell makes my jaw quiver.

"No, Liv! You're not supposed to smell it!" She giggles, and I follow with laughter.

"Okay, let's get it over with then."

And we both swallow the disgusting liquid. I don't take the time to taste it, I just force it down, even though it's trying to come back up.

"Ugh!" I groan and shake my head, blowing out the fumes of the jet-fuel that I just swallowed.

"Get used to that and we will have you drinking 'shine in no time." A male voice rumbles through my chest. I spin in my spot and find a boy; one I've never seen before. Sadie starts laughing.

"Olivia Hayes drinking moonshine? That will be the day." She grins and I cough away the remaining burn, taking a sip of the sweet wine in my cup.

"Liv, this is Sam, he just moved here a couple weeks ago. Sam, this is Olivia." Sadie introduces us and I smile widely at the tall, brown headed boy. His brown eyes are warm, like melted chocolate.

"Nice to meet you, Sam. I didn't realize that we had a new student." I look from him to Sadie.

She shrugs and makes her own drink. "Your nose has been in your books, Liv. Welcome back to the world, sister." She nudges me with her elbow. Sam laughs and his smile is soft.

No dimple.

No 5 o'clock shadow.

No danger. Sam seems like a safe person. Sam seems like somebody I could have a life with. Somebody my age and not a murderous asshole.

Jesus, Liv, you've known him for literally *5 seconds.*

"So, Sam, do you have an older brother named Dean?" I raise my brows, and notice how heavy my eyes still feel. "Does somebody here need saving? Any vampires to decapitate or bones to burn?" I ask, gesturing out into the air to nobody and nowhere in particular.

Sam's smile widens. "A *Supernatural* girl."

I only raise my cup to him in response.

"Seems like you two are acquainted enough," Sadie says into her cup as she sips. "I'm going to go find Ryan. I'll catch you before I leave so I can take you home! Love you! Have fun!" And she skips away, leaving Sam and I standing by the table. More people begin to step around us and I realize that we are right in the way of everyone making drinks so I direct us away, heading towards the fire. Sam follows right behind.

"I've heard a lot about you, Olivia." He says when he catches up to my side.

I tilt my head toward him. "Hopefully all the bad things."

He regards me mischievously, and the realization of how that sounded hits me. I cringe internally, my free hand pressing against my temples.

"I just mean that..." I breathe in deep, take a sip, and hold my hand up in surrender. "I've always been known as the safe person or a prude and I just don't want to be known for that anymore."

"I see," he says, the flames begin to dance in his eyes as we near the fire. "I think you seem okay. You're certainly not either of those tonight." He grins.

I turn my head to look at him.

"Do you want me to find us some chairs?" He turns to look around. There are a couple that are vacant but I shake my head.

"I'm fine standing here; I've been relaxing for like three hours. I smoked *the weed* for the very first time." I nod very matter-of-factly.

His eyes widen in surprise as he shoves his hands into his pockets. "Did you? How do you feel?"

"I feel alright. I've taken about six, or seven…maybe eight sips of this drink, too, so I'm sure that's making me feel differently. Oh, and I took a shot!"

He only laughs, and it's cute. I watch how his eyes crinkle at the corners and his lips curl up with his smile.

I wonder what Jackson laughs like when he's not being *Jackson*.

Dangerous waters, Olivia. We just spent a month trying to put him out of our mind.

My head shakes quickly and I find those hot flames.

"So, *Sam*," I drawl his name out. "Where did you move here from?"

"Washington. Seattle."

"Mm…" I take a sip. "I'm a Florida girl through and through. I don't like anything that's *cold, or wet.*"

He's quiet for a moment and I turn my head to find him grinning at me.

"You should try a harder one than that."

I can't help the smile that spreads on my face and I raise my cup towards him. "If the opportunity arises, I'll try my best."

"So, *Olivia*," he mimics me. "What are your life goals?"

"Woah, big question for a first date." I say, and then smack my hand over my mouth. "Oh, my God, I didn't mea—"

"This is a first date?" He interrupts my mumbling into my palm.

"No, obviously not, I swear it's only because I'm intoxicated right now."

Sam's warm brown eyes regard me for a moment, then he smiles and turns to look around him. "Stay right there." And then he disappears around the fire, returning a few seconds later with a foldable chair in each hand.

He sets them up side by side, careful to keep it a safe distance from the fire so we don't get too warm.

"Sit, my lady. I will procure refreshments."

I do as I'm told, collapsing into the chair and I fold my hands over each other, awaiting his return.

He is charming. He doesn't appear to be dangerous. He speaks my lingo, which means he's watched my movies and shows. That is kind of cool.

And his eyes are pretty. They sort of resemble my lighter brown, but his are darker. They certainly don't demand the same respect and fear that Jackson's do.

Jackson is a different person though, I'm sure that Sam is from the opposite side of town.

"Hear ye, hear ye," Sam's smooth tone reaches my ears before he rounds his empty chair and hands me a full plate. My eyes roam over the mountainous food as he speaks. "Nacho dip with chips, some baked beans, a cheese burger, and some…" he picks up one of the charred hockey pucks, "chocolate chip cookies?"

We both burst into a fit of laughter and I realize, that this is the most relaxed I've been in a while.

"This will help the munchies and mellow you out, just in time for you to drink some more if you wanted." Sam tells me. I nod and thank him as I take a few bites, silencing our words for the first time since I saw him.

He seems like a proper country boy. Plain white t-shirt underneath a loose blue and white flannel. Wrangler jeans and some off brand boots. His messy brown hair is perfectly windblown and carefree.

His boyish features and sparkle to his eyes tell me that he's experienced less life than he wants. He's a dreamer, a romantic, and he wants to see the world. Whatever my theory is, I know that Sam is night and day difference from the man who haunts my dreams. And nightmares.

"Why are you staring at me?" Sam finally asks after swallowing his food, and then looks up to me, stunning me into silence.

What am I thinking? Am I Dr. Phil now? I just stare at him for a minute and I know who he is and what he wants and all his desires?

Fucking idiot.

My mouth gapes like a fish and I finally spit out a word.

"Admiration. I—I, I was just admiring you. Not many people look like you and are interested in the same things I am. Do you read, too?" My word vomit spills out of me, and his eyes continue to twinkle.

"I do."

"Tell me what you like to read." I wait, not daring to breathe.

He looks down and sets his plate on the ground.

"Well, I love science fiction, but I love historical fiction, romance, mysteries. Anything with words, really."

"Oh, that's amazing. I only know of one other g—" I begin, but stop myself.

International territory, Olivia.

"Not everyone agrees with my philosophy of reading. Not everyone's had to escape their world like I have." I finish, hoping that I didn't just accidentally dump any trauma on him.

He only smiles at me. "I agree totally."

I wait for him to say something else, but I begin to feel a bit awkward when I find myself waiting longer and longer. When he doesn't speak again, I swallow and ask another question. "What's your last name, Sam?"

"Winchester." He grins and reaches down to pick up his cup.

"Ha! Good one," We both take a sip of our drink and he eyes me over the rim. "I'm serious, though."

"Gilbert."

"Sam Gilbert," I echo purposefully. "Samuel?"

"Samson." He corrects.

I raise my brows and purse my lips. What an unusual name. "Samson Gilbert. It's my pleasure." I hold my hand out and nod my head in a half-cocked curtsy.

"The pleasure is all mine, Olivia Hayes." He smiles so beautifully that it is *almost* breathtaking.

Sam downs the rest of his drink and sighs satisfyingly when he's finished.

"What would you say to going on a ride with me?"

CHAPTER

Eleven

"*Did you do this on purpose?*"

Jessie, my mother's fling at the time—who just so happened to be a trust-fund baby and a man child that had no direction—walked in on me in the bathroom that day.

"I'm asking you a question, Olivia Charlotte Hayes! Did you do this on purpose?!" My mother screeched again, her voice on the verge of bursting my eardrums.

It wasn't a regular walk-in-on-someone-in-the-bathroom, though.

I had just turned thirteen. School sucked. Other girls were assholes. My mom was a bitch. I had no other family, besides Nana. I would make stories up of my father for comfort.

Often, I thought about suicide. I thought that my mother's life would be so much easier if I'd just done it. I wanted to badly to just stop hearing her bitching. I never wanted to hear that I wasn't good enough, again. I only thought about it, though, because, let's face it—I was too chicken shit to do it.

So, what do people do when they are too scared to actually kill themselves, but still want to feel like they have that control?

They harm themselves.

I chose with a blade, and, it wasn't the first time I'd locked myself in the bathroom to do it, but my timing was off, and Jessie came home earlier than expected.

My mind still reels over how he got into the bathroom. I must not have locked it as good as I thought.

Fucking idiot, Olivia.

He walked in and froze when he saw me sitting on the edge of the bathtub, in my bra and underwear, little red lines of blood racing down each side of my thighs.

I froze when I met his eye contact, a blade between my fingers, mutilating my skin. He only looked from my eyes to my fingers to my thighs and the blood there, and back to me. Bouncing, back and forth, back and forth. I thought I might explode from fear.

After the longest thirty seconds of my life, I began to open my mouth to say something, but he only held his finger up for me to not say a word.

I didn't.

He took a step backwards.

Then another.

Then another.

And I never saw him again.

"No, Mom, I didn't. Don't worry about asking if I'm okay, or asking why I was doing what I was doing!" I yelled back at her, my emotions completely drowning me.

I wished they'd just get it over with.

The contempt in her features twists my heart in the worst way. No daughter ever wants to see her mother look at her that way.

"I didn't purposely look like a psychopath in front of your emotionally stunted man-child boy-toy!"

"I don't care, honestly, Olivia. I don't give a shit about what you have going on in your life, right now. You just cost us a place to live!" *My mother sneered at me, her liquor-laced breath fanning my face from where she sat in the driver's seat.*

My mother had just left the strip club, and she had picked me up from Sadie's on her way home.

"I'm sure. You should have just given me away when I was born if you don't give a shit if I live or die. We always have a place with Nana. You know that. Your boyfriend leaving shouldn't be my fault." Nothing could stop the shake to my voice, nor the tremble in my bones.

She slammed her hands against the wheel. "But it is! You go and do that fucking crazy shit cutting yourself in the bathroom and look! He's gone!" She reached down to pick up a cigarette out of the open pack in the cup holder. "Great job, happiness police! You make everything so un-fucking-happy. And as far as Nana goes," a humorless laugh escapes her, "I'll be on death's doorstep before I set foot in her house again." She spits her venom at me and lights her cigarette.

The tears in my eyes flowed freely. What can I say to that?

What did I ever do to make her hate me so fucking much?

"You know, you hate life so terribly, I make this shit so hard for you, don't I?" My mother asked sarcastically. I picked up my eye to look at her.

"You hate me and you hate that you're alive so how about this, how about I take care of both of your problems and end this now?" The mania that dripped from her words was unmistakable.

I knew my mother was psychotic, but that didn't excuse her words, and it definitely didn't justify the sinking feeling in my gut as I felt the car's engine begin to work harder.

"W—W—What are you doing, Mom?" I asked her and look back through the windshield.

She had said she had some things to take care of in Cedar Key, so, there we were, hurling down that two-lane road with woods on each side.

The speed limit was posted at 55 MPH, but I leaned over to see her topping 90 MPH, with a very sharp bend in the road approaching.

A realization washed over me, that my mother was going to attempt to end her life, and mine.

My heart thundered with the power of a category five hurricane. I thought that my heart might arrest before we hit the woods.

"Mom! Slow the damn car down!" I yelled, my hands finding anything sturdy that I could grab hold of.

"This is me giving you your gift, Lottie. I'm sorry that I have been the shittiest mother of all time. Maybe in the next life, I'll be better." Her words finally had an echo of regret, but it had no effect in calming my pulse. As we neared that bend, with our speed still increasing, I knew in my heart and soul, one thing for sure.

I did not want to die.

Against all better judgement, and many, many objections, I'm buckled up tight in Sam's passenger seat.

My heart beats against my ribs as I recall that dreadful night when I thought I was going to die at my mother's hands.

I obviously didn't. We were saved by some invisible force that I can only call God. Both of us made it out with only a few scratches, and my mother claimed that she swerved when she saw a deer, when questioned.

The police believed her and didn't give me a chance to speak. Not that I wanted to.

At that point, I was grateful to be breathing, and I would endure whatever I needed to in order to keep it that way.

But, now, sitting in this passenger seat, with a rumbling engine beneath my ass? This feels a lot like I deserve whatever happens for being the idiot that I am agreeing to this.

"Just relax! Everything's going to be fine." Sam grins at me as one hand grips the steering wheel and one grips his gearshift.

I'm putting my life in the hands of a young boy driving a stick-shift on dirt.

Lord have mercy on me.

The dirt road in the field leads to another field that is completely cut down, and it looks to be about five acres of openness.

The crowd of people line up and down the runway where the race begins. The road illuminated by our headlights and the full moon overhead.

Four other cars are lined up next to us, two to my right and two to my left. To my right is Dalton in his car and Kyle in his, they grin at me and rev their engines when I look at them. To my left is a boy I don't know and then one of the triplets at the other end.

This is the worst rendition of *Fast and Furious* I've ever seen. I shake my head with disgust of myself.

Why did I agree to this?

Any weed that I smoked, any alcohol that was in my system, is completely gone. It's been replaced with nerves and adrenaline.

And before I can even take another breath, we are in motion. I didn't even see anyone tell us to go!

Sam whoops and hollers next to me, mixing with the growl of his engine. I look to my right but don't see either Dalton or Kyle. I look to our left but only see Sam.

"They just don't know how we do things in Seattle, Loca!" Sam beams as he shifts gears again, the rumble vibrating my bones.

Even in the midst of not being able to breath, I almost smile at his *Twilight* reference.

He rolls the windows down and my long, untied hair begins to fly around.

This is…fun?

A laugh escapes me when I realize that every other car is well behind us. I look in the side mirror and only see dirt behind us.

"Oh, my gosh!" I exclaim, another laugh bubbling out of me.

"See, I told you to relax." Sam grins and he downshifts, obviously out in front of everyone else.

"This is incredible!"

And it really is. I never knew that feeling this rush could be so…invigorating.

And then we hit pavement, dropping my stomach to my feet. My eyes fly to his that sparkle with excitement.

"That was the easy part, now it's time for you to hold on, because this race doesn't end until we hit Buie Park."

Buie Park?! That's on South Side! Before I can even think of the technical directions, my bones get sucked to the leather seat behind me as Sam floors the gas.

I pivot to try to look out the back window and I see a few sets of headlights come into view off the dirt road, all of them well behind us at this point.

I just shut my eyes and I count.

I count seconds.

I count minutes.

I count how long it's going to take until I die.

We race down the back road that leads back to Highway 19, and we are still several miles outside of Chiefland's city limits, equal to Buie Park.

"Hold on, we are running it!" Sam exclaims and I open my eyes for a second to realize that we are not stopping at the stop sign before we cross over 19's four-lane highway.

Sam's car practically goes airborne before we get to the other side of the road, back onto another back road. I think of the interconnecting road adjacent to Buie Park and I believe I know exactly where we might be going.

"Scared yet, Loca?" Sam grins at me and I look at him with wide eyes.

"I've been scared since I agreed to this madness." I mutter to myself.

He only laughs and whoops some more, the wind still whipping around us and the night autumn air chilling my skin and bones.

We pass the road that I thought we'd turn down, and go further down. The next stop sign is the last chance to get back to Buie. And I feel like I've gone into something that I can't get out of, because I know that once we hit that stop sign, there's only one thing that stands between us and Buie Park.

Dead Man's Curve.

Oh, *shit*...Is Samson Gilbert *insane*?

Many lives have been lost on Dead Man's Curve. There's yellow signs and countless reflectors warning people of the oncoming turn where the speed limit drops down to 35 MPH.

Sam bends the corner at the stop sign and doesn't slow down, sliding onto the next paved road. The trees overhead shield any of the moon's light from hitting the road, the only light provided is the LED lights from Sam's car.

A set of eyes reflect back and I realize that there's a herd of deer ahead off to the right.

"Sam...there's deer. There's deer!" I reach out and grab his shoulder. An image of the sweet doe that died before me flashes in my mind.

"It's okay, Liv. You don't slow down, they don't spook. They only run when the engine changes, the noise is what freaks them out. Stay one speed and they'll stay where they are." He explains calmly as we hurl towards them, and sure enough, they are past us before I can blink.

How fast are we even going? I lean over to look at the speedometer, but Sam grabs my shoulder and pushes me back into place.

"I'm only slowing down enough to make this bend. You should probably close your eyes."

The yellow reflectors approach fast and the warning signs speed by me, and I remember Sam's words to close my eyes.

So, I do.

I squeeze them so tightly that I see stars in the darkness behind my lids and I feel the weightlessness when we skid around that curve. I pray and I hope and I trust in that invisible force that there's no cars coming around the corner, and that we might just make it out alive.

It feels slow motion; like how Lightning McQueen watched Doc Hudson bend that corner. Sideways and all.

"Woo-hoo!! That's right, baby! Fuck yeah!" Sam's yells finally reach my ears and I realize that I can open my eyes when I don't feel like my body is suspended over the asphalt.

We are back on the road, right where he intended for us to be, heading right to Buie Park.

He slows his speed, because I think he will reach it before the rest of them do, and I only smile as I feel those butterflies flapping away at my insides, reflecting the adrenaline.

"How was it?" Sam asks when we pass Buie, stopping for the last red light in town.

"Exhilarating." I answer truthfully. "I thought we were going to die several times." The shaky breaths that leave my lungs are full of

"But alas: we live!" His wide smile makes me laugh, and I nod my head in agreement.

"Yes, we do. The other guys must be way back there." I point out, not seeing any lights in the side mirror.

He shrugs. "They probably got caught by the cops. They'll be alright."

We go through the red light and travel the small road before getting back onto Highway 27, and returning to the party.

I wonder what Sadie is going to say whenever she finds out what I just did. She would be so proud that I'm living. A sense of pride warms my chest, or maybe it's just the remnants of the alcohol and weed in my system as I come down off the adrenaline high.

Sam passes under the webbed entrance again and we stop at the long line of rowed cars.

"Thank you, Sam, that really wa—"

My words are cut short when the passenger door is ripped open and I'm out of the car, being held by one arm around the waist.

"What the hell! Put me down, psychopath!" I scream, but it's to no avail, as I'm hurled over the person's hard shoulder. My fists pound at their back, and that overwhelming scent clouds my mind.

Jackson Fucking Wolf.

CHAPTER

Twelve

*J*ackson practically throws me down into a different passenger seat only a couple steps away and I her Sam's voice before he shuts the door.

"Yo, what the fuck, dude?" Sam calls out, his head poking over the top of his silver car. Jackson takes pause, and then turns to look at him slowly.

I know the look. I've seen it. I've gotten it. A silent command. A wordless threat. Sam says nothing else as Jackson slams my door with me inside.

Confusion clouds my mind. He preaches to me about staying away from him and my group of friends. I've done what he asked. The first time I let myself have fun, this is what he does? As if he's my father or my keeper?

I take the small moment of him stomping around the back of his car to look around the small space. It's clean, a lot cleaner than you'd think a man's car would be. And it smells like him.

Leather, cigarettes, and coffee.

Jackson slings open the driver door, jumps in, and is peeling out of the clearing before he even has his door shut. It's evident that his frame is rattling with rage.

Rage for my safety? Or rage because I was with another guy?

"What the hell—"

"I don't want to hear a word out of your mouth, Olivia!" His thunderous voice clamps my mouth shut.

His black hair tumbles across his forehead, long enough now that a few loose curls have formed. The muscle in his jaw flexes as he grips the steering wheel.

He looks no different than the last time I saw him on that stormy and emotional night. The mere sight of him makes me feel like I can finally breathe again.

Am I crazy for that?

"Where are you taking me?" I ask, my voice a lot smaller than I intend for it to be. I don't fear him. Only scared of why he's acting this way.

"Home. Where you should have been all night." His words are clipped and I scoff, a little disappointed by his answer. The last place I want to be is *home*.

"So, what? You're my father now? Newsflash, I have been fine my entire life without one, so *fuck off*!"

He flashes me the darkest look I've ever seen from him, and in a split second, I'm worried that I might catch the shit end of his wrath.

"I'm not in the goddamn mood for your eccentrics tonight, so please, *shut the fuck up* and let me get you home."

"Oh, you're not in the mood? How about, I'm the one not in the mood! You just physically removed me from the fun that I was having!"

"Yeah, I can tell. You smoke, you drink, and you climb into a car with a guy that you just met to *race cars*? *Really fucking smart, Olivia*. You're doing exactly what I told you to do. Once again, blurring that goddamn line." The sarcasm drips from his words as his speed accelerates, going the same route that I just went with Sam.

It's the exact opposite of what he asked me to do. If I weren't intoxicated, I would have never made that choice. Sober Olivia wouldn't be so stupid.

A blurred line between bravery and stupidity.

Jackson brings his free hand to his forehead and he presses against his temples, that muscle still dancing in his jaw.

"Fuck, Olivia!" Jackson bursts. I jump when his hand smacks against the steering wheel. "Do you realize how fucking stupid that was?" His words are almost strangled. "I've *killed men* for following lesser orders than 'just stay out of trouble.'"

It's so strange to see him so unchecked. The Jackson that I met and have seen is so self-controlled that the way he's acting seems a little unhinged.

I whip my head to face him. "Well, if you haven't noticed, Jackson Wolf, I'm not one of your little soldier boys that want to kiss your ass if they piss you off."

And, then, I'm grateful for the seatbelt that I'm wearing as he stomps on the brakes, his car skidding to a stop.

"Oh," Jackson chuckles, "You haven't pissed me off." An acid storm brews in those green eyes, the intent very clear in his demeanor as he leans into me and towers over me, even in a car. "You have fucking enraged me, Olivia. I gave you a direct order—"

"I'm not yours to order around!" I cut him off by yelling in his face. My chest heaves and my breathing is heavy, my own rage fueling my outburst.

His features are hard when his eyes rake down my neck and sheer sleeves of my shirt, and stop on my exposed belly. When I tried on the shirt, I had tried to imagine what Jackson would look like if he saw me in it.

My imagination has nothing on the reality of it.

Jackson gives no evidence of liking my outfit, but there is *something* in his eyes.

"You get high, you get drunk, you go to a party with your friend Mercedes—the girl I told you to stay away from—, you meet a boy and hop into his car without a care in the world." His words are calm now, and deliberate. As if he wants me to understand everything he's saying. "These reasons, are why I asked you to stay away from Mercedes. You are too green to see dangers when they are looking you in your face."

I listen to his words, but I don't move, our faces inches apart. I'm silent for a few moments as his last sentence resonates with me. A few images of the men that raped my mother flash by. A few more of the trees that I saw before my wreck. Other horrendous things I've experienced with her.

I've faced many dangers in my life, too many for him to tell me I'm *green*.

And then I refocus on his face, the one that's staring so intently at me, so close to my own face.

Landon's warnings echo through my mind.

"What about you? Aren't you a danger? You are quite literally looking me in my face."

His nostrils flare for a moment and his eyes find my lips for the smallest second before returning to his seat, leaving me utterly bereft. My lungs push out a breath at his absence and he returns to pressing the gas, and returning to our ride.

"I've always been the danger, Olivia." His words are soft, too soft to have come from the anomaly that is Jackson Wolf, and there's not enough air in the car to breathe through his intensity.

I turn to find the trees passing us by and I remember that first day on Pole Cat when I met him, the feeling that I had in my chest.

I've always been the danger, Olivia.

Has he been protecting me from himself?

Jackson Wolf having a heart?

We pass over Highway 19 and are on the road that leads to my house, and I dreadfully anticipate him dropping me off.

"You are so smart, Olivia. You are diminishing your light by simply being around your friends. They will not be with you when you excel at your life. You deserve so much better than what you are getting."

I blink a couple times and look to him and his stern features. "There's nothing wrong with my friends."

Jackson chuckles. "Landon is on a bank run out of state right now. Mercedes is currently getting fucked on the hood of a ninety-seven Ford pickup by one of those ginger triplets. And you, were cross-faded sitting in the passenger seat of a car with a kid you don't know and put your literal life in his hands."

I pause before responding, a little shocked at his lack of secrecy with Landon, more shocked at his knowledge of Sadie— because, I mean…come on. Who would know that? —and acceptance of his description of my actions of tonight.

But I decide to overlook all of that.

"He knew what he was doing." I almost chide.

"And that," Jackson holds his finger in the air, "is exactly why I say you could never survive the lifestyle I live. He barely kept his tires on the road. You're lucky to be alive."

My palms rub against my jean-clad thighs, ridding the perspiration. It really was a dumb move. I knew I shouldn't have done it. For more reasons than Jackson scolding me.

"Is he one of your guys?"

"Who?"

"Sam. Samson Gilbert."

The muscle in Jackson's jaw raises. "No."

"No? I thought you ran this town." It was supposed to be a joke but it came out serious, earning me a less-than-enthusiastic look.

"I do, Olivia. This kid must be new and not run in any circles. People like Samson Gilbert are the reason I've been telling you to stay far away. I don't know him, and…" Jackson takes a breath and speaks again. "There's a war coming."

That feels…ominous.

"A war?" I whisper.

"One that you need not be anywhere near. You have a different life to live, and you're going to live it."

How can somebody be as cold and heartless as Jackson Wolf spew words to me that sound an awful lot like he cares about my well-being?

What if…What if I didn't want to live my different life yet? I have an entire year before I leave Florida. What if this the only time in my life that I get a chance to feel what it is to be cared for by somebody?

I'm so lost in the what ifs and the overwhelming intensity that seeps off of Jackson that I don't realize that we are sitting out in front of my house. The low, idling rumble of Jackson's engine amplifies the anxiety that tumbles around in my belly.

I don't want to get out.

But I have to, apparently.

My hand reaches to pop open the door, but I feel warm, rough fingers against the inside of my left wrist. I stop and turn my head to find Jackson a whisper away. His eyes hold me captive the same way that they did the first time I saw him.

"I know that I'm an asshole, and my way of doing things is brutish, but I'm not trying to be either when I tell you that you can't have any part of the life I live. The things I'm involved with, the things I see…this life would absolutely tear you apart." I find myself watching his lips move when he pauses to lick them. My eyes lift to his when he continues, and I have a moment of absolute clarity, just him and I. "You are pure. You are good. You deserve the life that you dream of having. The dark world we live in has nothing for you, Olivia. I mean it when I say that this life would rip you apart, and I might not always be there to pick up your pieces and put you back together."

My breath hitches in my throat at his words. At the implication that he would so long as he's alive, and I disregard the butterflies I feel at his kind adjectives of me and focus on one statement.

"But you would?"

"I would what?"

I hesitate to ask the question, to actually say the words rattling around my brain. "You would pick up my pieces?" I take a breath and look down to how our arms almost touch. "And put me back together?" My eyes find his again, but they quietly study my face, roaming over all of my features, as if trying to commit them to memory. After a few moments, he captures my gaze again.

"If there were anything left of you, yes. I would." And then he pulls away, settling back into the driver's seat. "I'll get your car to you. Try to make good choices."

The word 'goodbye' doesn't seem to live up to everything that I want, and probably should, say, but my mind is clouded by the mysterious aura that encompasses Jackson Wolf.

So, I wordlessly exit his car and shut the door behind me. My feet carry me around the front and as I step onto the soft stones of the walkway to my front door, I hear his window roll down behind me.

"Goodnight, Olivia Charlotte Hayes." Jackson calls to me through the night air.

"Goodnight, Jackson." I whisper back, and he drives away, leaving me standing there dazed and with a cloudy mind.

CHAPTER

Thirteen

"For life and death are one, even as the river and
the sea are one." – Kahlil Gibran

*I*t's never occurred to me how fast death can occur. You think
of cancer and how long it takes to finally rob someone of their
soul. You think of bleeding out, and how long it takes for all the
blood to finally be gone, that essential life force flowing away
from its host.

But really, it's that final second. That split moment where
one's heart stops that is the finality of death.

I've experienced loss, in a sense, when my mother left.
I've experienced grief, in a sense, over my father and never
knowing him

But I've never experienced loss and grief paired together over
any given person dying.

Until now.

A week ago, I was celebrating the holiday of all things
spooky.

Today, I celebrate a life lost.

"...and Lord we gather here today, to celebrate the life..." Pastor Clark's voice drones in and out as I stare at the black casket that's sitting on the ground in front of the rectangle hole that's dug six foot deep.

It's staggering just how quickly life can, and does, change.

Being a week into November, with the subtle weather change, hurricane season still brews strong, and there's one sitting in the gulf, strengthening as it sucks up the warm water, getting ready to dump it all on us.

However, it's still cold. The cool little water droplets that hang in the air make me hug my arms to my body as tight as I can, but it doesn't soothe the never-ending ache in my chest.

I'm reminded of a time in my childhood, with my best friend.

It was a rainy day, a category three directly overhead. The district hadn't closed the schools, because the storm was only supposed to be a tropical depression. Overnight, and unexpectedly, it strengthened. And Chiefland was about to be slammed with the eye wall. The howling winds whipped around the old building, and thunder rumbled the foundation.

We were directed to line up along the walls of the hallway, with our backpacks on our back to cover our heads if need be.

I was seven years old, and utterly terrified. Sadie's parents kept her home, in fear of this happening. My mother forced me to attend, no matter what.

So, although I was lined up with my classmates, I felt completely alone, squeezing my eyes shut to block out those whining winds that rattled the windows in the classrooms.

Until a hand touched mine.

My eyes popped open to find the owner of the hand, and was relieved to see Landon next to me.

"It's going to be alright, Liv. We are in this together!"

My eyes refocus, my chest aching. I remember how grateful I was for the security of his friendship.

I place my hand to my breastbone trying to rub that ache away thinking about how much I'd love to have that same friendship right now.

I suck in a breath, expanding my lungs, hoping that it alleviates only a fraction of the torment that I feel when I think of how much I'm going to miss him—more so, how much I *already do.*

I blink away the fresh wave of tears for my fallen friend as I try to listen to Pastor Clark.

"…such a beautiful soul that was taken way too early. He was a friend to many…"

A friend.

Landon Williams was more than a friend. He was family. I think back to all the times he took care of me when I was sick. One time in particular sticks out above them all. It was the time when I knew Landon's feelings for me went deeper than platonic buddies.

My fever was at 103.2 and wasn't budging. I had chills and cold sweats bundled up beneath my comforter. Nana had called him; she knew that I'd rather have his calm spirit over Sadie's.

He'd brought chicken soup, blue Gatorade, and a bunch of Mark Wahlberg movies. We watched movies for hours, and laughed, and stayed bundled up underneath that blanket.

But it wasn't until it was nighttime and I'd fallen asleep after my fever had broken, that I felt his fingers brushing my forehead and running through my hair. I was so exhausted from battling such high temperatures, that I thought I was dreaming it.

I know now that Landon had loved me for far too long than I deserved it.

Pastor Clark continued. "Landon was a son to…"

A son.

Landon's father stands front and center, not a tear wetting his face. His stepmother stands next to him, cradling her barely swollen belly. And his mother…

Landon's mother stands directly opposite of her ex-husband, and she looks exponentially worse. Her pale, translucent skin and sunken cheeks and eyes are telling signs that the cancer is going to take her soon.

I'm sure she wishes that she would have gone sooner rather than feel the pain of losing her only son.

Ryan, and Ryan's father, who is Landon's uncle, stand beside the rest of their family, also expressing their pain by way of tears and sniffles.

"We pray that Landon's soul has made it safely home to you, Lord, and we pray for peace for the grieving friends and…"

Grieving friends.

I turn my head to my left, Sadie's red-rimmed eyes tugging at my heart again. My eyes look out, scanning the crowd.

There are hundreds of people. Classmates, teachers, administrators, family, citizens from the community, even people I've never seen before. Nana is here somewhere, too.

"…don't know why these things happen, Father, only You do, so all we can do is…"

Guilt.

My mind and heart have been heavy with the suffocating feeling of culpability.

Could I have convinced him to stay on track and help his mother some other way? Would he still be here if only I'd loved him the way that he loved me? Would he have changed his ways? Just like my mother said after that awful moment with those men, *'if you'd have tried harder.'*

Pastor Clark finishes praying and in unison, everyone says "Amen."

Landon's father steps up to the podium to give his eulogy, but the look on his face is enough to send me over the edge.

His fake pain.

So, I turn and I break away from the crowd, hoping that nobody follows me.

This funeral is a joke. Nobody here knew the real Landon, and nobody here would lend a hand if they had. He needed real help; his mother *still* needs help.

It's bullshit, the way everybody is standing around, crying for him.

I finally shove past the last row of people standing in black and the air feels smoother, like it's easier to breathe.

Landon's family has plots at Orange Hill Cemetery in Williston, about thirty minutes away from Chiefland. So, here we all are, in our Sunday best, anticipating the hurricane's arrival. The angry skies overhead begin to announce his presence with thunderclaps and whipping winds.

As we say our final goodbye to Landon Williams.

My head tilts back as it starts to drizzle, and I look towards those grey skies. A deep breath fills my lungs in a fruitless attempt to soothe that ever-cracking chasm in my breastbone.

My best friend is dead.

The next morning after Halloween, I woke by nothing in particular, but I wanted to sleep desperately. Exhaustion still was heavy, but I couldn't shake the feeling of dread. Something felt...wrong. My stomach was in knots for no reason.

About an hour passed before my phone started ringing and I stared at it for a few moments before picking it up.

4:19 AM.

Sadie.

And I knew in my bones that something terrible had happened.

Sadie's scream was so blood curling that I thought she was being hurt. I was on my feet in an instant with my stomach in my throat.

It took her several tries before she could get out that Landon had died.

I'd just seen him. Didn't I? When was the last time I'd talked to him, even texted? I couldn't recall.

I ran to the bathroom and threw up everything in my system. I couldn't stop heaving, my muscles straining to toss my pain out with it.

Landon was dead.

The thought wound me up so tight that I thought I was going to explode. It didn't make any sense.

How could he have died?

What happened?

Nobody knew anything yet. My mind reached for the conversation I'd had with Jackson.

"Landon is on a bank job out of state right now."

Did that mean he was robbing a bank? I didn't think too much of it when he'd said it, and I wished I had a way to talk to Jackson when it's not just on his time. I needed to know what happened.

It wasn't until the next day that I'd found out.

On the record, Landon Williams died in a car accident involving a drunk driver. He was vacationing in Destin Beach, Florida and was t-boned on his way back home.

Off the record, Landon lifted a package off of a group of guys that had just robbed a Bank of America right across the border in Alabama. They followed him back to town and ran him down right outside of Tallahassee. Landon's father paid the county enough money to cover up the fact that he had twelve bullets in his chest.

I don't know if anyone else was with him, he was the only casualty.

My brain to tells me to go get in my car and go home, but home is the last place I want to be right now. I have been holed up there for a week, not wanting to see or talk to anyone. Even Sadie.

I know she's struggling, too. Landon was her best friend as much as mine. But she seems…debilitated. Like someone stole the air from her lungs and hasn't let her have a particle of oxygen. Maybe I'll get to see her after everything's calmed down and we can have a real conversation.

After all, it *is* just us now. Shouldn't we stick together?

My feet carry me all the way to the tree line, making the remaining distance to my car very short, and I scan the entire cemetery. It's almost completely full.

My eyes land on a shadow in the distance, back at the furthest part of the cemetery, and the person is too far away to confirm, but I know that it's Jackson.

Always watching.

Always waiting.

Always knowing.

I want to blame him so badly. I want to call him a murderer and turn him in and rip him apart.

But this…this life—or lack-thereof—is exactly what Jackson told me that he wanted me to stay away from. That it would tear me apart. This pain, this crippling pain, is what he didn't want me to feel. Or worse…be the one in that casket just for being around the wrong people.

I hate him for being so…right. It's obvious Jackson has many years on me, and I hate that he has that wisdom. He saw this before it happened, and I thought he was just being an asshole.

I don't think that Jackson had anything to do with it. He and everyone may act like he's this hard-ass, but he's shown me otherwise. In his gift-giving, in the softness of his touch…in his eyes. The past week has been a sort of hell for me. A torment like one I've not ever known. And every time I find myself receding into that dark space of my mind where I don't want to feel it anymore, I wish that I had his arms around me like they were the night I hit the deer.

Especially at night, when I'm terrified to go to sleep, I wish that I could bury my face so deep in his chest that all I know is Jackson Wolf.

So, with an aching soul, I stand here and I stare him, knowing that he's watching me. I'm sure he knows I'm watching him.

The rain picks up with a clap of thunder, and I lose him in those rain drops, turning my focus back to the mass of people beginning to rush out of the rain.

And before I turn and start for my car, I spend one last second looking at Landon's casket and the dark earth that he will be lowered into, praying that one day, I might see my best friend again.

When I arrive home, I'm surprised to see that my grandmother's car is already home, in the garage, and more surprised when I see Sadie's car parked in her usual spot off in the grass. I pull up in my spot, right in front of the stone walkway leading to the front door.

The lights in the kitchen and living room can be seen through the rain, and I made the run inside on my tip-toes, careful not to splash too bad.

I'm met with the nutty aroma of warm coffee and something sweet...banana bread?

I push the front door shut behind me as I shed my soaked black hoodie and my black sneakers.

"...definitely remember that. He was dressed with that wig on, and was it your actual cheerleading outfit?" Nana's voice carries through the foyer and I announce my presence.

"Nana? Sadie?"

"In the kitchen, Liv," Sadie calls back to me and continues her and Nana's conversation. "Yes! It was," she laughs softly. "I can't believe it fit him, either. He was a great sport about it, too." Her voice sounds like her normal bubbly voice, but when I come into view, the curve of her slumped shoulders is telling me something entirely different.

Nana is in between the oven and the island, leaning on her elbows, a half-empty cup of coffee in front of her. Sadie sits with her back to me, turning when Nana looks up to me with sad eyes.

I look away too quickly. I've cried enough in the last week, I'm over it.

"Love you, girls," Nana says solemnly. "You two have to stick together, now. I'm going to my happy place; you know where to find me if you need me."

Nana squeezes my shoulder as she walks by. I'm not much of a hugger, and she's always given me that space and respect. When Nana says she's going to her happy place, she means that she's going to take care of the animals. It calms her since my grandfather died...like she's got a connection of a sort with him.

"How long have y'all been here? I left when everyone else did." I walk around the island to take Nana's spot. I don't opt for coffee, though. I'm just…not in the mood. I do, however, grab a knife and cut a piece of the banana bread from the loaf, picking up pieces with my fingers.

"We left right when it started raining, right about when Landon's dad started talking." Sadie responds, running her finger around the rim of her mug.

"I figured it must have been early. I didn't even see y'—"

"Liv, I have to tell you something," Sadie cuts me off, and I swallow my bite and hold my breath.

CHAPTER

Fourteen

"What is it?" I ask cautiously.

Sadie crosses her arms and places her elbows right on the marble countertop, taking a deep and stabling breath.

"I have lied to you, and I've been lying to you for a long time, and I thought I would get the chance to do this before…" She trails off and blinks the fresh tears away from her eyes, her hand reaching up to swipe them away.

A knot of uncertainty forms in my stomach as a wall begins to build itself. A wall of protection around my heart. I can't handle anything else after Landon dying.

I stay quiet, though, waiting on her to tell me whatever it is.

"I don't know any other way to put it, so I'll just…say it." Her eyes cast downward and she chews on her lips for a moment before looking back to me.

"I loved Landon."

I blink. "So did I."

"No…" Sadie shakes her head. "I loved him like he loved you."

My brows raise in surprise, but my mouth just hangs open with no response to be had. That's a bomb, not just a secret. But still, a little confusing. I thought Sadie had a thing for Ryan, not…our best friend.

"I always have, but he's loved you, instead." Her words are full of sadness, rather than envy.

"Sadie, I…" I what? What is there to say? *'I'm sorry'*? That doesn't suffice in the slightest. What would I even be apologizing for?

She shakes her head again and offers me a small, sad smile. "There's nothing to say, Liv. I'm not mad at you, and I don't hate you. I've just…always loved him. And, the miscarriage that I had…it—it…"

"It was *Landon's* baby?"

I didn't think my jaw could fall any lower, but it absolutely can and does. How do you describe the feeling when you find out that your two best friends were sleeping together? And they made an actual baby? I don't know how to. But it *feels* an awful lot like betrayal. How long has this been going on?

"Liv, I know that you are upset. We both knew that you were going to be. We weren't really 'together' though." She air quotes 'together' as if that's going to make me feel any better.

I want to yell, and every bone and muscle in my body pushes me to do that. But, I'm just…utterly shocked. And confused. How could they have pulled this over on me? Why wouldn't they tell me?

My mind throws me back to the Homecoming game when they both humiliated me, and the look that they shared after. And I begin to think of all the times and all the moments when they looked at each other for a little too long, or Landon's hand rested on her knee and then yanked away too quickly when I saw, or when their hug was a little too lingering.

"How could I not have known, Sadie? You're my best friend! *He* was my—" But all words leave my mind and all breath leaves my lungs, my mind completely caving in on itself. A constant whispering reminder of the massive elephant in the room.

Landon is gone.

I suck in a breath to ease that ache and my feet begin carrying me down the distance of the island and back, pacing back and forth.

"He had always hoped that you'd wake up and love him back. He didn't want to come out with us because…well…" Sadie searches for the words. "Landon didn't want to be with me. I was just…there. Always available. Always his. And he was waiting for you."

"Sadie…" I say, stopping at the sink with my back to her. I look out into the rainy night sky, the lightning from the house softly illuminating the front yard. What do I say? What do I even feel?

"I have so many questions. I feel so many things. But I think that I need a little bit of time to sort this all out." She is silent as I keep my back to her and I begin again. I say with a shaky voice, "I know you're grieving, probably more so than I am, given what you just told me. But I need some time to just… *breathe.* And think. And understand."

My back stays to her, not wanting to let her see the massive alligator tears welled up in my eyes.

I'm so hurt and angry, that I don't know what to do at this moment, but continue to stand here and look out into the dark, watching the rain fall.

Sadie's chair scrapes the tile and she takes a breath, pausing before speaking. "I love you, Liv. I'm here whenever you've had enough time."

In a few seconds, the front door opens and closes, and I'm left alone with the remains of the grenade that was just dropped on me.

She came here after the funeral of our best friend. She told me she's been sleeping with, and conceived a child, and miscarried that child, with the same best friend. And then she left.

How could she drop something on me like that? This feels like it felt those few days I spent in bed after the game.

I should have known then that they had something going on. I should have *known*. How could I have been so...

Naïve? Blind? Innocent? What is the right word to explain the shittiness I feel?

Fucking stupid.

I think back to something Jackson said. That my friends don't deserve my loyalty? Did he know about them? Did Ryan know? Was she sleeping with both of them? Did Sadie know about Landon's mother having cancer? Did she try to stop him getting involved with Jackson?

So many unanswered and unending questions that are pouring in that I just want to shut it all off. I want to power down and not have to think about Landon or Sadie or Ryan or Jackson.

I don't want to feel anything.

This is the overwhelming feeling that I had as a teenager. It's all so much.

So many emotions.

Oh, how desperately I wanted to just *not feel it anymore*.

I sigh and hang my head. I need a shower. And I need to sleep. That is the only thing that will help me right now and clear those awful thoughts.

Numbly, I carry myself through the kitchen, down the hall, up the stairs, and to my room. Nana must not have gone out to the animals, because I can hear the television playing in her room at the opposite end of the hall.

As much as Nana tries to act like nothing bothers her, and she keeps a good attitude about everything, she is taking Landon's death as hard as the rest of us. She watched him grow up and fed him when he was having a hard time with his father. I'm surprised that she skipped her animal chores for the evening, though. I can count on one hand all the times she's done it.

I'm grateful for the woman. She has given me too much grace than I deserve, especially with everything that I've been through and dragged her through consequently.

I sometimes wonder what life was like with her and my mother. What if she had never lived the life she did? Where would she be? How did she get to where she is? Nana is an amazing grandmother. What happened for my mother to be so absent?

Life is so incredibly short and here she is, squandering it.

I take another breath, one like the others that really aren't ever deep enough, and turn to my bedroom, trying to shake off the compounding misery.

As soon as I turn the doorknob and take a step inside my room, I know that something is off. All thoughts of Landon and Sadie and pain have evaporated and I'm hyperaware of this feeling.

Somebody has been in my house.

In my room.

The hair on the back of my neck stands up as I freeze in the doorway. My eyes scan my area, but nothing looks out of place.

A pile of the clothes still sits on the floor.

My bed remains messily made.

A few pair of shoes sit scatters over by the closet.

Nothing's wrong, but something is different.

I take a step in and still look over my room, from the closet to my dresser, by the window, and I stop when I get to the desk in the corner of the room.

Something sits on top of it that wasn't there before I left for the funeral earlier.

A small package wrapped in brown paper.

I sniffle and clear my throat as I carefully approach the package, the strangest feeling stirring low in my belly.

Jackson was in here. Before I saw him at the funeral, he was here.

How did he get in?

My fingers run over the brown paper and it's wrapped exactly as the first time, in the shape of a book, but a lot smaller.

My heart is exhausted, its heavy beating evidence of that, but beating, nonetheless.

I take the package in my hands and tear at the paper, revealing a thin…journal? The front and back covers are black and hard. I flip the cover to reveal a scribble on the first page, and I hold my breath as I read it.

Olivia,

There really isn't much to say to someone in your position. "I'm sorry" could never suffice. However, please know you aren't alone.

Grief is a lot like the ocean. It's deep, and it's blue, and to our finite human minds, it's bottomless. Its tides come in and go out, the good days leaving us feeling elated and the bad…immeasurably painful. When it's high tide and you feel like you're drowning, write. Find solace in putting it on paper. Find solace in finding yourself again, even after this tragedy.

You are strong. You are beautiful. You are deserving of everything you dream of. Don't let this shut you down.

Until fate overlaps our paths again.

- J

My lungs deflate as that breath bursts from them. I read his words again, and again, feeling them cut into my core each time.

My fingers thumb through the white pages, its edges painted gold and its lines thin and black.

"Beautiful," I whisper out to nobody at all, and feel those tears that I've been desperately holding back slip down my cheeks.

"Thank you," I whisper again, and bring the cover to my lips, pressing a quick kiss there.

It is strange, how quickly I disregard the fact that Jackson broke into my home and literally invaded my privacy. My soul clings to the idea of him putting his heart into something like this.

For me.

However, less than a year, and I'll be starting anew.

And that deafening reminder is exactly why I should shut the yearning down. I don't need to keep my head down and suffer until I leave. I will do what I've always done, and I will be strong and I will continue on, just like Jackson said I would the last time I spoke to him. This gesture was just him being kind, and I'm so grateful for it.

Landon wouldn't want me to turn into a depressed human being. He'd want me to forgive Sadie and go on with my life.

I set the journal down and begin getting ready for bed. With my eyes heavy and my mind sluggish, my body goes through the motions, and before I know it, I'm tucked in under my comforter.

And it's the first night that I fall asleep without crying in a week.

CHAPTER

Fifteen

"*Do you see, Lottie, why we don't trust men? Look at where we are. We are sitting here because men are untrustworthy.*" *My mother slurred to me, crossing one leg over the other.*

We were sitting on a park bench, two suitcases side by side; one for her, one for me.

It was my fourth birthday, and the only man that I'd known my mother to be with had kicked us out, from what I understood, was because she cheated on him.

It's screwed up how a four-year-old can understand what that means.

But she did *work at a strip club, so he shouldn't have been too broken up over it.*

They'd never married but he was like a father figure for the first couple years of my memory. He'd take me for ice cream. I think he took me fishing a couple times. He was kind to me.

And my mother was a bitch to him. She was a bitch to everyone that looked her direction, especially me. I often would hope and pray that she would be nice, just for today.

It was always a fruitless attempt.

"*One day, when you are old enough, I'll tell you how I ended up this way. I hope you don't follow in my footsteps and turn out*

like me. That's a mother's worst fear, her kids turning out like her."
She plucked a cigarette from the pack and lit it to life.

I didn't understand those words when I had such a small mind,
but I knew they felt sad. I felt sad.

I think I felt sad my entire life. There were times where I would
be happy, and it was fleeting, because I knew that it would never
last. Something would always happen and things would always be
sad again.

My mother hated crying though, she hated any sign of weakness,
and instilled that in me. She refused to let anyone see her as a weak
soul, and she didn't want to see me weak. So, she made me hide it.

"All of this that we are dealing with," she waved her cigarette
around in the air, "all of this bullshit, is to keep you safe, Lottie.
One day, one day you will realize that. I know I'm a horrible
mother, and I know your father wanted better for you."

My four-year-old mind didn't realize it, yet, but my mother
was crying. She was being vulnerable for the first time, in front of
me, and it would be the last time that I ever saw her shed a tear.

"But, just know this: no matter what you get into, where life
takes you...love isn't real. Because if it were, we wouldn't be where
we are right now."

I didn't know if she was referencing the man that just left her,
or the man that broke her heart years before, but either way, that
was the first and last time that my mother ever spoke of my father
and what he wanted.

"Happy birthday, Lottie, baby." She slurred, and that's the last
thing I remember from my fourth birthday.

It's been nineteen days since Landon left this world.

Twelve since we've laid him to rest.

Twelve since I've seen Sadie.

I've not reached out to her, still trying to work the bullshit out in my mind. I miss her but I hate how blind I was. How stupid she made me feel.

I've not seen Jackson either…I have no way to get a hold of him, and without Landon…we live completely different lives and our paths have no reason to cross. His journal has set on my desk this entire time. I've tried to sit down and write, but I only am ever able to get the date onto the paper. Every word I think about writing just…hurts. And I end up longing for that embrace that I know he can provide, that understanding of my pain. So, I always end up shutting the book and turning back to my bed.

I took the first week off school and work to just vegetate between the sheets and I think I cried every drop of hydration out of my body.

Now I'm left with this open wound that's just…numb.

After the funeral, I collected all the work that I'd missed from school and returned to work, but continued to take off school, just doing the work from home. With only three classes, and one of them a study hall, there's not much that I can't do off campus to make up the work. The school board decided that—seniors only, since Landon was a senior and they didn't want every single person abusing the rule—we could do our work from home up to a month after Landon's funeral.

I mean…how else does anyone deal with a death? It's gracious of them to give those of us close to him the time to grieve without worrying about faking a smile for people that really don't matter.

I've grieved. I've spent a better part of three weeks grieving, specifically preparing for today.

Saturday, November 19th.

My eighteenth birthday.

I knew this week would be hard, because Landon and Sadie and I always do something on my birthday. Adjacent to that, Thanksgiving is this week, as well.

Two holidays that I loved celebrating with my best friends.

It's so insane to me how fast life changes. Everything was good, and then, it just...wasn't.

While preparing for today without them, I've also been preparing for yet another birthday without my mother.

No, she probably wouldn't be pleasant to be around, but...is it wrong of me to miss her? Even with the wall I've built to keep her out? After everything that I've gone through, is it awful of me to hope that she's changed?

Here I am, entering a chapter of my life that is supposed to be liberating, and exciting, and a breath of fresh air.

Instead, I'm alone, and I'm suffocating, and have become a slave to the memories of my best friends.

So, what I planned on doing today, in this order:

Wake up.

Eat breakfast. Something easy—pancakes?

Shower.

Dress.

Go to town and get three Redbox movies.

Go to Walmart to get snacks.

Come home.

Get into bed.

Binge and binge.

Sleep.

It's foolproof. Nobody will bother me, and there's nobody to pretend for. Nana knows I'm down bad right now, so she hasn't bothered me much. She's made sure I'm fed and hydrated and rested, and that's the most she can do right now, and she knows it.

It's a sunny morning, and I've eaten and showered and dressed, and now I'm ready to walk out of the door, waving Nana goodbye.

Everything is going according to plan so far.

Except, as soon as I open the front door, there is someone standing there, their hand up and ready to knock on the hard wood.

Both of us are surprised, and I take in the stranger's features. *It's a woman.*

Her hair is completely grey, and sort of thin and stringy, cutting off right past her shoulders.

Her clothes hang off of her body as she drops her arms to her sides.

Her face is sunken in, her cheekbones protruding.

Her skin is yellow.

Her eyes are dull and almost lifeless.

There's no car behind her, and only one bag sitting by her feet.

The woman in front of me gives me a strange feeling of nostalgia, but doesn't resemble anyone that I know, so I offer an awkward smile and turn to tell Nana that someone is here, until I hear her croaking voice, tainted by years of smoking.

"It's so good to see you, Lottie. Happy birthday, baby."

A tsunami of realization hits me as I take in her once-familiar features again, and I'm stunned into silence, only able to stand there and stare at the woman before me.

My mother.

CHAPTER

Sixteen

I've thought about this day for four years.

I've wondered how I would feel when my mother finally graced me with her presence again. How would I react? I hold so much hate in my heart for her and her ways, but how everlasting is it if I were already wishing that I might see her on my birthday?

Does contempt have an expiration date?

I thought I would be mad.

I thought I would be raging, completely distraught that I'm even laying eyes on her again.

I told myself I'd never forgive her when I realized that she wasn't coming back.

I didn't think that she would be in the state she is now. The only thing that I can do is stare at her with my mouth hanging, like an idiot.

I certainly didn't think that I would feel pity for the woman that's never, ever pitied me.

But, just like that, I reach my arms out and pull her into me, feeling eighteen years of built-up resentment just disintegrate, blowing away with the autumn winds.

I hear Nana's footsteps round the corner and I pull away from my mother to turn and look at Nana. Her face shows the same initial confusion and then realization.

"Allison?" Nana's voice is a lot smaller than I have ever heard it. She wipes her hands on her purple apron and approaches us slowly.

"It's me, Mama. I'm home." Once again, that raspy-ness of my mother's voice catches me off guard. Her entire appearance catches me off guard. She looks even older than Nana.

A soft cry leaves Nana as she joins us on the front porch, pulling my mother in for a hug in the same fashion that I did.

"Oh, my sweet, sweet girl." Nana cries. "I can't even begin to tell you how relieved I am to see you again. I thought you'd died, Allison. Oh," she cries again, eliciting the tears that I didn't want to shed today, "thank you, Jesus, for returning my baby to me." Nana's eyes are squeezed shut and her arms hold on for dear life, as if my mother might slip away again.

Am I still sleeping? Is this made up?

I can hardly believe this is happening. My mother, right here before my eyes. A tidal wave of emotion slams into me and a quiet sob leaves my mouth as I lean down to pick up my mother's bag.

Nana pulls away and ushers her inside. I set her bag gently on the couch, my mind reeling. Where has she been? What has she been doing?

The more pressing question—*what happened to her?* Why does she *look like this?*

My mother that I grew up with was a bombshell. Every man she met followed her like a lost puppy dog and now she looks like…like every drop of her youth has been sucked out of her. The last memory that I have of my mother, her hair was solid black and she was full of life.

"Are you hungry? Thirsty? Can I get you anything?"

My mother only shakes her head at Nana and runs her fingers along her eyes. "I just can't believe I'm home. It's been so long."

"Yes, it has." I say, but with more attitude than intended. There she is...that anger.

Her blue eyes find mine and she offers a sad smile. "I'm so sorry, Lottie. I—I..." My mother shakes her head back and forth and continues. "I don't have an excuse for leaving you here, other than I realized that you deserved better than what I was giving you." Tears well up in her eyes and she fully faces me. My nerves begin to quiver, my hands shake, but I only have the ability to stand there.

Are we really about to do this? Right here, right now?

My lack of response pushes my mother to continue. "I'm not trying to give you a cop out. I'm being honest with you." Nana reaches out and grabs my mother's hand.

"How about you tell us all about it over a cup of coffee? Come, let's get you settled in, here."

Nana ushers my mother into the kitchen, getting her positioned onto the high stool. My feet absentmindedly carry me around the corner, still not believing that she's here.

There is a bout of awkward silence as Nana makes the coffee. My mother and I sit in the stools next to each other and I...don't know what to say. Or do.

When I was younger, if I were just sitting in the kitchen like this, I would often hear something along the lines of *'Lottie, you would lose a lot more weight if you'd stand up instead of sitting all the time.'*

I shake the memory away and refocus on the seemingly changed woman in front of me.

"Okay, darling, here you go, just how you used to like it." Nana sets a cup of coffee down in front of my mother and sets one in front of me as well, shooting me a smile.

My mother sips from her mug and hums slightly. "Thank you, Mama. This is delicious."

I think I'm too nervous to drink mine, leaving it sitting there, waiting on my mother to say something. Anything.

"Anyways, I guess I should start from when I left," My mother flashes me a nervous glance and she brings her hands together to rest in her lap.

"First, I just want to say, again, that I'm so sorry, Lottie. The entirety of your life, I've known that you deserved a mother like I had growing up, and I'm so deeply sorry that I wasn't that person for you."

I only nod softly and swallow down the lump forming in my throat.

"When I left here, I travelled. Visited different states, went to clubs, I really lived." Her eyes go distant as if recalling a faded memory. "And after about a year, I checked into rehab. A beautiful place in Napa Valley, of all places."

"You were in California?" I'm not sure why it matters. It is comforting to know that she spent some time in the same state that I'll be living.

She smiles and nods. "I was there for two years, fully cleaning out and learning how to live without any substances or alcohol."

"That's amazing, Allison. I'm so proud of you for that, honey." Nana praises with bright eyes and I reach out and grab my mother's hand, her hopeful blues lock on our contact for a few moments.

That is quite a feat, if you knew who she was when I was growing up.

She doesn't look away from our hands together as she speaks again. "And I went through really intense counseling. A lady that helped me come to terms with so many things in my life… including you." Finally, she looks to me, and I swear that I can feel the walls continuing to fall down each second we spend in each other's presence.

"I've worked hard to heal, I've worked hard to become a woman that you would be proud of, someone you might even forgive and respect as your mother. I wanted to put down all the booze and drugs and I…I realized, far, *far too late*, that I'm ready to be here. For you."

I remember thinking to myself that I wanted to be someone that even my mother would be proud of. I guess we aren't so much different, after all. A warm sensation spreads through my chest, constricting my lungs.

My mother pulls her hand away from mine, and I swipe the perspiration against my jeans.

"And…this is the part that I've been dreading to talk about. I know we are moving kinda fast but, I just want to get the important parts out and if either of you have any questions, we can go from there." She says, with a nervous and breathy laugh. "I checked out of rehab and I started having some health problems."

Nana shifts behind the counter and clears her throat, and I sit, frozen, waiting. This must be why she looks the way she does.

"H—Health problems?" Nana asks cautiously.

My mother nods. "I'm sick, Mama. And, I wanted to come home and make peace with my family before it's my time."

Nana's chest deflates with the news and her hand flies to her mouth.

"What do you mean you're sick?" I ask.

"I mean…" My mother blinks a few times. "I have stage four pancreatic cancer. No treatments have helped or will, Lottie. I *am* going to die. And very soon."

The tears in her eyes match my own, and I think that I might actually pass out.

I'm still in shock that she's even here and now I have to grieve her all over again?

I'll ask again…am I dreaming? Is this a joke?

"So, you leave for four years and you decide it's a good idea to come back into our lives to *die*? Do you have any idea what we have *been through*, Allison?" Nana's voice holds a tremble that I've never heard from her before, but if I had to guess the origin? I would say it's coming from rage.

"Well…I—I—"

"No, you don't. And, by all means, please don't give a damn about what *I've* gone through, it's not a daughter's place to worry about her mother's well-being. But you? You leave *your baby* here and now you come back in time for her to *watch you die*?" Nana's defense stirs long-stuffed away emotions and I clear my throat, shifting uncomfortably. It's almost refreshing to see Nana's anger. I know I'm not alone in the emotion.

"*Your baby* just had to bury her best friend. A boy she's grown up with her entire life, she had to put him in the ground and say good-bye to him forever. *Nineteen days ago, Allison.* And she had to do it alone, because her mother wasn't here to hold her through that god-awful pain." Nana's index finger jabs the air at my mother, and the only thing that my mother can do is sit there and take it. She doesn't fight back, she doesn't object, she doesn't shake her head or try to defend herself. She only sits there, her hands crossed in her lap, and looks at Nana with a reverence that I've never seen my mother have.

Like she's finally accepting the reprimand that she's fought so long her entire life.

"This…this…this…" Nana shakes her head rapidly and her chest rises and falls. "You *didn't think* to call me before you just showed up like this?"

My mother only shook her head softly. "I thought it would be a surprise," she turns to regard me softly, "for Lottie's birthday."

"Well, it ain't *my* birthday, Allison! God Almighty…" Nana begins to pace the length of the island for a few moments. "I can't believe you would be this thoughtless. Olivia has experienced enough heartache to last a lifetime, and here you are, just dumping more onto her!"

"Nana, it's really f—"

"Lottie, I'm so sorry that you are going to go through this. If I had any say in this, I would have told her to bear her crosses alone so you didn't have to experience two of the most important deaths of your life all in your last year of high school. You deserve better than this." Nana tells me earnestly, and doesn't skip a beat. Her eyes bounce between my mother's and mine a few times before she looks down to the counter.

"I need a breather. Lottie, please help your mother get settled in the spare room." She nods toward us and then leaves us in the room, in our deafening silence.

"She's right, baby, I'm so sorry." My mother attempts and when her voice cracks, I stand to my feet,

"M-mom, it's not something we have to talk about right now. Let's get you up in your room. I'm sure you're tired from your trip."

I leave her in the kitchen as I retrieve her bag, and head up to put it in the spare.

Nana had the right idea. A breather is much needed right now.

Once my mother gets into her room, she lays down and its only seconds before she is fast asleep. I stand in the doorway for a few moments, watching her chest rise and fall.

It must be a side effect of the cancer for her to fall asleep so fast.

How soon will it be before the sickness consumes her? How long do I have to make things right? What if I'm not ready before its time? What if I'm too late?

So many questions, so much uncertainty comes with my mother arriving back in my life at this rather inconvenient time. Nana was right. I just buried my best friend. And to go through the pain of another loss in such a short amount of time…Will I be able to handle it?

Am I strong enough to go through this?

I don't have long to think on the question when my phone vibrates in my back pocket.

> Sadie: Happy Birthday Bestieee!!! I'm not sure
> if you have plans today but I'd love to take you
> to supper and a movie if you're down.

I drop my hand after reading the text and look over my mother once more. She will probably be sleeping for a while, so I decide to meet Sadie.

If there's anything that I learned since I woke up a couple hours ago, it's that life is very short, and don't waste a second.

I was angry with Sadie. I took my time to stew. Now, it's time to let it go and make up with her. We are all we've got through this pain of losing our best friend.

So, I shoot a quick text back and turn on my heel to go get in my car.

CHAPTER

Seventeen

*M*y mother is already asleep when I arrive back.

For this, I am grateful. Sadie and I went to eat Japanese food and caught a new movie.

We had a small talk over dinner, but it felt all wrong and different. Honestly, I had quite a hard time focusing on anything except the fact that my mother is back.

And she's dying.

That small reminder kept sneaking back in and stealing any fun I was having. As soon as I'd begin smiling and relaxing, I would remember.

My mother's back.

But she'll be dead soon.

It was incredibly exhausting to keep a smile on my face after that.

I decided not to tell Sadie about my mother. That she's back or that she's dying. I would just honestly rather not talk about it. I barely even talked about the situation with us. All I said was that I forgive her for lying to me, and we went on with supper.

As I finish brushing my teeth, I tap the brush on the side of the sink and drop it into its cup. I find my hair brush and yank it through my wet hair, flipping on my hair dryer to assist in drying the long and thick locks.

Looking back on it, I think that I just wanted to get out of the house and didn't want to spend my birthday alone. Sadie offered so I took her up on it.

The movie was good, I think. I don't remember much of it.

I wish Landon were here. We always did the dinner and movie gig, even if Sadie couldn't come. My heart twists but I choke down the tears. I've cried enough today with the return of the prodigal mother and her news of one foot in the grave.

My thumb flips off the dryer when my hair is finished and my feet carry me into my room to get dressed. A black t-shirt and some sweats suffice.

It's not too terribly cold, even this late in November. A heat wave came through and is warm enough to not wear a sweater out.

Comfort, though. Comfort is my goal. My whole body cries out from exhaustion.

How much more of this can I take? My soul feels as if it's taken lashings.

I sip from a water bottle as I pad over to the window, looking out over the front of the property. It's dark, so there's not much to see, except the hues of purple over the horizon slipping into the deep blue of night. There's no moon tonight, no light to look out over the animals. I can barely even see the driveway.

Except, off to the farthest left of my window, there's a tiny flicker of light. It's so small and quick that I almost miss it.

But I don't, and I don't ignore it. There's nothing over on that side of the property that would give off any light, sparks or otherwise. The animal pens are to the front and back of the property but not on the sides.

My eyes squint as I strain to see if it comes again, and there's no flicker again, but there is a small red glowing dot. It gets brighter and then softer, and after a few moments, brighter again. Like a cigarette.

Someone is out there.

Jackson?

My heart begins to pick up pace as I step out of my room. I take a peek inside my mother's room and then Nana's, both of them snug in their sheets.

One step, after the other, I skip some steps as I race down the stairs.

My feet slide into the plastic flip-flops that I keep at the French doors leading into the back yard, and I quietly slip out into the night.

It takes a moment for my eyes to adjust to the darkness and I find the side of the yard that I saw the light, realizing that the gazebo is out there. It's overgrown with jasmine and honeysuckle, so it's pretty much a vine structure. Only the entrance is visible in the shape of a dark oval.

How was I able to see the light?

My footfalls crunch against the dry grass and I slow as I near the structure, my heart beating rapidly. What if it's not Jackson? What if it's a stranger or a crackhead camping out here?

I approach the gazebo slowly and clear my throat to announce my presence to anyone there.

Am I fucking crazy? I can see my headstone now. Olivia Charlotte Hayes, died on her birthday for being an idiot.

"Happy Birthday, Olivia." That deep, smooth, and velvety voice grabs my attention and sends chills over my skin.

Am I delusional for being relieved that I get to see him on my birthday?

"Jackson?" I whisper back, holding my hands out to navigate in the poorly lit area. There's nothing but woods behind the gazebo.

"The one and only, baby." I can hear the smile in his voice and I smile back, not trying to push down the butterflies tickling the inside of my belly.

"How did you know it's my birthday?" I ask him, stepping foot inside the gazebo. Once inside, I realize that the vines are only thick enough to destruct the view inside, but not out. Small slivers of light shine in from the barely-there-moon and the flood light on the corner of the house pointing this direction, illuminating features of Jackson's face.

The hint of a smile graces his lips, where my eyes linger. "There's not much I don't know."

"Well, thank you," I breathe out. "For wishing me happy birthday." My arm reaches out to feel around, and I catch his hand.

Abort, abort, abort.

I yank my hand away but he reaches out to pull it back to him.

"How did you know I would see you out here?" I question, enjoying the way that our fingers are so gently, and effortlessly intertwining. He sits on the high bench, his legs swinging softly back and forth, and our hands rest against his jean-clad thigh.

The pads of his fingers are rough enough to scrape the soft parts of my hand.

"Well," Jackson begins, pulling on the end of his cigarette with his free hand. "I'll let you in on a secret." He blows the smoke away from my face and pulls me closer, bringing me to stand between his knees. Our sheer closeness has my heart racing with the strength of a thousand mustangs. "I've been here every night since Landon died."

My heart practically stops. All the nights that I cried myself to sleep. All the nights that I wanted an end to the pain. He was here.

"But why?" I whisper.

He hums as he smashes his cigarette against the wooden bench, snuffing it out.

"I guess I'd just hoped that you'd want silence, and find refuge in this gazebo."

With you.

"I'm sorry that I didn't—"

"You've no reason to apologize, Olivia." He cuts me off. We are so close to each other that I can feel his warmth radiating, warming my skin to levels they've never reached before. "Like I said in my note to you, you're not alone in your pain. Landon was a good kid. He had good reasons for initiating. He was my recruit." That never-ending ache reappears at the mention of Landon. And a realization hits me that Jackson has been dealing with Landon's death just like me.

Is that why he was waiting here every night?

Jackson's thumb swipes gently across the back of my hand, eliciting a breathy sound from my lips. His eyes watch me intently. "How was your birthday?"

My birthday? *Oh. That.* Obviously, I'm not going to tell him what a fucking doozy it was.

I take a deep breath and let it out, looking down to where our hands touch. "It was alright."

"Olivia," Jackson's voice demands my attention. My eyes snap to his and I hold my breath. "What did I say about lying?"

What did he say? My memory reaches and lands on the time outside of Connor's.

I chew on the inside of my lip, the angst making my head swim. I barely made it through the day, I don't want to tell him about my mother and all the bullshit that came with her.

Jackson presses the pad of his thumb to my lips. "Stop doing that," he demands softly, his eyes fixated on his thumb against my lips, "and tell me how your birthday went."

"I-I—It honestly was awful." I say, the image of my mother's sickly state brings that damned emotion, clogging my throat. Tears try to well up but I blink until they are gone again.

"You don't have to hide from me, Olivia. Whatever is going through your head...*feel it, and let it out.*"

As if on his demand, the tears spring to life, spilling over my cheeks. I try to blink them away but Jackson reaches up and wipes them. "There you go. I knew today would be rough for you."

My bottom lip quivers and I shake my head.

"It's not just Landon..." Another wave of tears floods my face and I sniffle. "My mother surprised me today. I haven't seen her in four years."

The words feel funny as they roll off my tongue, but I keep going, despite my pain trying to choke me up. Jackson's eyes regard me softly as I speak, his hands holding mine between us.

"And the worst part about that is...she was gone for all that time, and yeah, she's back, but...she's dying. She has cancer and it's going to kill her."

That part doesn't feel as bad saying it out loud. Is that because I've already braced myself for truly being without her for so long?

Jackson stays quiet as a few soft cries leave me. He pulls me into his chest and his hands run over my back. That damn intoxicating scent of his makes my head swim.

If anyone else were standing in front of me, I would *never* be showing this side of myself. But…when it comes to Jackson Wolf, I find myself questioning all of my morals and beliefs, every ounce of will-power going out the window.

"It's just shitty, you know? That she was such a shit parent, she disappears, and then comes back reformed. Like, she would actually be a decent mom for the first time in my life. And then…she's just…going to die. Alone again."

That's what hurts.

That I've been alone my entire life, and the first chance that I get to have her, she's ripped away by uncontrollable forces.

My arms wrap around Jackson's waist and I press my cheek against his chest. One of his hands brush the fallen hair from my face and I can feel his fingers running through the strands, flush against my scalp.

He does this over and over again, as if coaxing the tears out of me, and I continue to cry into his chest, unable to soothe the ache in my heart over my mother's impending death.

"I'm so sorry to hear this, Olivia." Jackson hums against the top of my head, driving that stake deeper.

The tears flow and I don't loosen my hold around his back, too comfortable with his arms around me. The way that his fingers slide against my scalp and down to the ends of my hair, over and over and over again, seems to calm the storm that is raging in my mind.

His touch is relaxing.

Calming.

Comforting.

My heart rate slows when he begins to speak.

"Losing a mother is arguably one of the worst things you can go through as a person. It's one of the worst pains to be felt, and the fact that you have to anticipate what that might feel like is..." I keep my cheek resting against his chest, feeling his deep vibrations down to my toes. "I wish that I could experience it for you, Olivia."

A certain warmth spreads throughout my being, the same way that it did when I stopped him from killing Landon that day. It's the first time that I've had another emotion besides pain since Landon died, and then, an even stranger feeling falls over me.

I don't want this moment to end.

"Thank you, for being here." I whisper, not trusting in my voice yet.

Jackson stays quiet for a few moments and his fingers still against the back of my neck, tangled in the roots.

"I shouldn't be here, Olivia. I'm still all the things you were told. Bad things tend to happen to the people that I care about," Jackson loosens his grip, running his fingers the rest of the way through my hair. "And if anything bad happened to you because of me? I fear the monster that I'd turn into."

Tingles. All the way to my toes.

"Cold, heartless Jackson Wolf *caring* about someone?" I finally pull away from his chest, placing my palms flat against his thighs. "I figured people in hell would have a slushie before that."

I try my best at a joke, and am rewarded with a one-dimpled grin, gorgeous enough to take my breath away. I can still see the warm green of Jackson's eyes, even in the poorly lit gazebo, and his hair is perfectly messy, hanging right above his brows. I wonder how soft it is between my finge—

"I don't want to ruin your life, Olivia." Jackson almost whispers as he presses his forehead to mine. "I should be letting you go so you aren't tainted by the blood on my hands."

He reaches up and tucks my hair behind my ear, his fingers trailing down my jaw. Our noses brush together and I breathe in the scent that I can only identify as Jackson Wolf.

Intoxicating in its nature.

"What if I don't want you to?" I whisper back.

His breath hitches as if he's relishing in the sound the words made coming off my lips, and he captures my chin. His other hand lands on my hip, the pads of his fingers slipping under my t-shirt and landing on my skin. I suck in a breath at the contact, and how warm his hand is against my bare flesh.

"I'd say that you might be as insane as I am." He chuckles, a low and dark, delicious sound that elicits a certain heat deep in my belly.

And lower.

"Maybe I am. So what?" I challenge, our lips only centimeters apart. I don't think that I even know what I'm saying right now. This is not the Olivia Hayes that I know. I reach up and wrap one hand around his wrist holding my chin, and my other hand grips his thigh in an attempt to calm my wild-running nerves.

Jackson hums his approval, sending another wave of that wet heat between my thighs and I think that my knees might give out when presses his lips so gently against mine that it feels like the feather-light touch of an angel.

It's over too quickly and he pulls away, pressing his lips to my forehead next.

Am I crazy for even being out here with him? It sounds insane. But these stolen quiet moments don't *feel* insane.

They feel like the most sane and clear-headed thing I've ever done.

"I have a gift to give you, before I forget." He says, reaching into his backpack sitting off to the side.

A gift?

Nobody got me anything today, and I think I might cry from his thoughtfulness.

When his hand emerges from the bag, it holds two items wrapped in brown paper.

"You like this brown paper, don't you?" I laugh and pull my hands away to grab it from him. He smiles as I take them in my hands.

"Well, I've never given anyone a gift. Ever. And I didn't think that the frilly paper at the store was you. So, I picked something versatile and that I could use for any occasion." His explanation makes me smile big, and I just shake my head and begin unwrapping the first one.

"No, do this one first." He says, pulling the smaller box from my fingers and handing me the large, heavy one.

I oblige and pull at the paper, revealing four books. A series.

It's almost too dark to read the titles, but Jackson helps me before I struggle too hard.

"This series is about a girl who got involved with a group of boys, and fell in love, and in the end, it changes her life in ways that's hard to imagine until you read it. It has loss, and grief, and government corruption, and love. I figured you might enjoy them." His words wrap around me like a cloud as I run my fingers over the spines. He has them tied all together with a string so they stay together in a stack, and my heart swells at the gesture. I can't believe someone as deadly as Jackson Wolf is giving me a set of books for my birthday.

"And these *are* my books," Jackson says as his hand covers mine holding them. "Don't let anything happen to them."

"I will protect them with my life, I swear it." I giggle and bat my wet eyelashes at him.

"Okay," he smiles and brings both of his hands to cup my face. "You're so beautiful, Olivia. Happy birthday."

"Thank you," I respond with tears in my eyes. "I'm sorry for crying. Nobody has ever…" I search for the words as his thumbs wipe the tears slipping over my cheeks.

"Understood you?" He finishes.

I nod and swallow. "Exactly."

He smiles a soft and knowing smile, presses a kiss to my forehead, and gently pushes me back to make way for him to hop down from the high bench.

"Next one." He demands, placing it back into my hands after I set the books down on the bench.

My fingers rip at the paper, wrapped around an oblong shape. The paper falls away and reveals a small…knife?

It's about six inches long, no longer than my hand from my palm to the tip of my middle finger. Its handle is solid black leather, and the blade is sheathed with the same black leather.

"Oh, my…" I whisper, tugging at the sheath. The sharp edge of the blade gleams even in the darkness and I wrap my hand around the handle.

A perfect fit.

"Do you know how to use it?" Jackson asks me, and I look up to him through squinted eyes.

"The pointy end goes in first?"

He grins at me and tilts his head to the side, gripping my hand that still holds the knife. He brings it up to the side of his neck.

"Here." He whispers, softly pressing the blade against the soft skin of his neck, right underneath his jaw.

He pulls our hands to his chest, directly over his heart and, presses softly against his clothed skin. "Here."

And then he goes lower, guiding our hands to between his legs. Panic takes over my mind.

What is he doing? What is he doing? What is he doing?

My eyes go wide and my fingers struggle to release the blade, but his hand is too strong, holding me in place. The edge of the blade presses firmly against the seam of his jeans.

"Here." His voice demands my attention to his mouth, and then he lets go of my hand. "These three points are the goal, but there are other places if need be."

A little dazed over the fact that I literally almost touched his dick, I clear my throat and nod, trying to seem like I'm not having a stroke.

I've never been so close to any guy before, but I won't pretend that I didn't love the anticipation.

"Head, heart," I say, checking off in the order that he went in, and, once again, I decide to make another joke. "*Head*. And if I want to know anything else, I'll watch a YouTube video."

Jackson pulls his backpack over his shoulders and he smirks, his eyes lighting up. "Anything you want to know, baby, I'll teach you." Literally, he means self-defense, however, I get the feeling that his statement has a dual-meaning.

"Again, I hope you had a happy birthday, Olivia." Jackson hums as he pulls me into his chest, his arms wrapping around my back.

"I did, thanks to you."

"Good. I'll see you here, same time tomorrow."

My heart skips a beat.

"Okay." I smile into his firm chest.

"Sleep tight."

"Okay."

"Good night." He whispers and presses a kiss to the top of my head.

"Good night." I whisper back but neither of us move.

"I'm not going anywhere until I know you're safely back inside, so, you might want to let go so that I can get back to work." Jackson's chest rumbles underneath my ear, and I'm immediately reluctant to let go.

But I do.

"I'll see you tomorrow." He assures me and I turn to take a step out of the gazebo.

"Promise?" I ask, taking another step.

"Pinky." He holds his pinky finger in the air and I chew on my lip to keep from laughing.

And before I'm sucked back into Jackson Wolf's gravitational pull, I turn and run back to the house with my gifts in my grasp. I lock the door behind me, and lock myself in my bed room the rest of the night.

It wasn't until I'd gotten to my room and buried myself under the covers that my eyes landed on the sheathed knife on my nightstand.

And the diamond encrusted "W" on the very bottom of the handle, making me smile like an idiot.

CHAPTER

Eighteen

Thanksgiving has always been my favorite holiday.

Turkey, ham, stuffing, neck-bone gravy, cranberry sauce, mashed potatoes, macaroni and cheese, sweet potato casserole, green bean casserole, corn casserole, seven-layer salad, corn bread, and rolls. Sweet tea to drink and five different pies for dessert. Apple, blueberry, pumpkin, pecan, and chocolate pecan.

Nobody does Thanksgiving like Marie Hayes.

Nana makes enough food for us to eat for breakfast, lunch, and dinner, for at least three days. She begins her prepping on Wednesday and I always make sure that I'm up early on Thursday to help her bake and cook. Like her little sous chef.

It's a good day to make memories, and Lord knows I don't have a lot of them. Thanksgiving is exponentially better than Christmas, because I never had the magic of Christmas as a child, and for Thanksgiving...you don't have to give gifts. All you do is eat and be happy with a full belly.

Happy and with a full belly should be enough for anyone.

This Thanksgiving is much, much different, though.

My mother had assured me yesterday that she would be up to help Nana in whatever capacity she could since it will, without a doubt, be her last time to do so.

That leaves me to lay here in bed, having just woke up, and smiling like an idiot, still feeling my skin tingle wherever Jackson's touched and kissed. I'm wrapped in his black hoodie that is absolutely massive on me, and...

God, it smells just like him.

The night after my birthday, he did return, like promised. He brought a candle so we could have some kind of light to see each other, which gave a sort of romantic aura to the shielded gazebo.

I'd began reading the first book of the series he gave me and almost finished it by nightfall. I raved and raved over it to him, feasting on the delight in his eyes as I did so. I asked him about his work and he avoided the question, telling me that "anything that has to do with his work could incriminate me as well."

He kissed me sweetly good-bye that night, just like he did the night of my birthday, and it left me feeling a little disappointed that he didn't go further.

The third night, Monday night, he brought burgers, fries, and cherry Coke from Ronald's, and we ate together beside the candle light. I continued my review on the series he gave me, having read more, even during work that evening. He listened intently and offered his thoughts at certain parts. When we were finished, and he kissed me goodbye, he lingered for a few seconds longer, telling me that he would be gone working out of town the next day, and would miss our meeting here, but would make it up when he got back on Wednesday.

Tuesday night, after I got home from work, I locked myself in my room and read all night until I finished the second book and began the third. It captivated me in a way that I've never been by a book before, and left me with tears and a broken heart. I finished the third book and read the last one in one sitting, resulting in me pulling an all-nighter. Reading is the only way that I didn't drive myself crazy wondering what Jackson was doing. What was so important that he had to go out of town for? The tale that he gifted me kept my mind busy enough to not fret over it.

I thought about all the concepts involved in the book, and was surprised that he would share something like this with me. The storyline is incredible. There's love, and there's death, and grief, and the innerworkings of a gang trying to bring down a government.

To know that Jackson let me have a glimpse inside his mind, inside the things that he enjoys, feels…incredibly intimate. I've gotten to see a different side of him in the last few days. How he laughs, and how his eyes have a gleam to them whenever he pulls away after kissing me, how his dimple pops out whenever he's trying not to laugh at something stupid that I said.

The Jackson Wolf that he's shown me in the past few days isn't the same Jackson Wolf that I met on Pole Cat months ago. I wonder just how long he's had to shove this side of himself away, hardening his heart to adapt to the life he lives.

To the lives he takes and those he loses.

Last night, he showed me just how much that darkness has hold of him.

I was waiting in the gazebo for him, ten minutes before our planned time. I'd brought a blanket out to lay on the wooden floor, lit a few extra candles on the rails around the edge, and set up cups of hot chocolate on the bench, some trail mix that Nana had made earlier in the day set aside as well.

The weather has dropped considerably since my birthday, just in time for the holiday, so I opted to wear a thick long-sleeve t-shirt and my usual sweatpants. I made sure to shower and shave and lather my skin in a new lotion that I ordered, jasmine and vanilla scented.

I waited for only a few moments before I heard the crunch of fallen leaves behind the gazebo, and they were at a fast pace.

My heart began to race as I set the books stacked up next to the cups and the snacks, anticipating seeing the only man to make my mouth water and my pulse pitter-patter.

He rounded the side and I turned to face and greet him, but he didn't have talking on his mind.

His hair was damp, like he'd just gotten out of the shower, hanging down in his eyes. But he had a busted lip and eyebrow, blood running down the side of his face and down his chin. Random dirt spots darkened his features and there was red staining his arms, coloring those shadowy bones. His eyes, though, remained bright and fiery.

Jackson Wolf that I met months before stood before me, and he didn't let me process the state that he was in before his hand hooked around the back of my neck and he crashed his lips onto mine.

He threw his backpack on the floor of the gazebo and he wasted no time. Jackson kissed me hungrily, and greedily, and didn't let me up for air until he pulled away to slip his tongue between my lips.

Tasting me.

Claiming me.

A twinge of iron flooded my mouth, and I could only assume that the cut on his lip was still bleeding, but that didn't stop him, as he continued kissing me, his breathing heavy.

He backed me up until the high bench was against my lower back. His knees bent, scooping behind my legs, and stood to set me on the bench. His hands slid around to my knees, pushing them apart so he could stand between them.

The kiss was all fire and passion. I'd never experienced lust until I met Jackson Wolf, and last night, he kissed me so fervently that if he were to ask, I would have given myself to him.

He pulled away long enough to take a breath and slide his hands up my thighs until they hit the bottom of my t-shirt. His fingers caught the hem, tugging it upward, but my hands flew to keep it down.

"Jackson, I'm—" I began but stopped when his blazing, and pleading, eyes found mine. "I'm only wearing this shirt."

"Do you trust me?" His voice was gravelly and enough to undo me completely.

The thought of being bare to Jackson made my head dizzy. Nobody's ever seen me naked and...

What if he didn't like what he saw? Or he eventually grows tired of it and leaves?

"Do you trust me, Olivia?" He repeated, that tone that demands a response had me nodding my head.

I do.

"Yes," I whispered out, and he hummed his approval before capturing my lips once more in a hungry kiss, leaving me breathless.

He pulled away again, his hands working to pull my shirt up and off my arms. The cold air sent goosebumps over my exposed skin, and hardened my nipples to a peak.

Oh, God, how embarrassing.

My hands went to cover myself but Jackson caught them, his green eyes feasting on my bare skin. A wave of heat blanketed me and there wasn't enough oxygen in the world to fill my lungs and calm my thundering heart.

"F-fucking..." Jackson breathed out, his words faltering. "You're so fucking beautiful, baby." He hummed, sending sparks to places that I didn't think possible.

He lowered his head, his wet lips landing on the exposed skin of my neck, eliciting a soft moan from me.

My hands found his hair, relishing in the feel of running my fingers through it as he leaves a trail of wet sloppy kisses down my neck. His warm hands roamed over my bare back and over my sides.

A jolt of pleasure shot up the very center of me as he pressed further in, and I sucked in a sharp breath in response.

"Jackson," I moaned out, feeling the highest I've ever felt.

I screwed my eyes shut when he pressed in again, a dark chuckle leaving him as he kissed further down, through the valley between my breasts. His mouth found one nipple and a noise that sounded like a squeak and a moan fell from me as I arched my back further into him.

He groaned as he pressed against me again, the sharpness of his teeth against my sensitive flesh almost passing me out. He pulled away with a popping sound and his fingers catch the other nipple, dragging another moan out of me and a dark laugh from him, fueling my fire.

The slight friction between my legs had me panting as his fingers rolled and tugged on my nipples in unison. My entire body felt as taut as a bow getting ready to fire off. He began to speak, low, and slow, and pressing kisses to the hot skin on my neck every few words.

"Fuck, Olivia," Jackson pressed a kiss to my jaw. "You're absolutely intoxicating." He pressed a kiss underneath my ear. "Watching you experience this for the first time." He pressed a kiss further down my neck. "Is unlike anything I've ever seen." He leaned into me, once again adding friction against my hot center. This time, he did it with a certain pressure as he rolled my nipples between his fingers, and he latched onto my neck, pulling a patch of skin between his teeth.

The three actions together made me screw my eyes shut and cry out...but not from pain. I felt like I was going to explode, and the stars behind my eyes were like blinding white light as I fell into that ocean of pleasure, my body convulsing as I rode those waves.

"That's it, baby, that's how you come for me." Jackson whispered against my neck, further adding to the sensation. "I've been thinking about watching you do that since I left on Monday night." He pulled away and his hands ran up and down my arms as I pressed my hands against my chest.

When I opened my eyes, I found him watching me, our faces only inches apart.

"Are you okay?" He asked.

I nodded, completely and utterly breathless, wordless, and thoughtless.

That was better than anything I've ever done—or had done to me. My sexual experience was in the negatives.

Until Jackson Wolf.

I leaned into him, pressing my exposed chest and belly against him to hide it from the chill. Every single muscle and nerve in my body felt spent. And sated.

My body fell back, resting against the soft-leaved vines of the jasmine. After that magic that I felt, even with those dark eyes on me, taking in every inch of my bare skin before him, I didn't feel the need to cover up or hide. I would have stayed right there forever, just so I could see that expression he had on his face.

One of awe, and desire, and rightness.

He shifted slightly and I felt the large bulge still between us. I looked up to him with wide eyes.

He smirked at me, those flames in his eyes not dying down in the slightest. "I know you're chomping at the bit to experience it all in one night, but I'll need you to slow it down, please, ma'am."

My mouth fell open to object but he shut me up by leaning forward and pressing his lips to mine.

"It was a joke," he said when he pulled away. He leaned down to his backpack and gestured for me to sit up. He pulled out a hoodie to put over my head.

The smell engulfed me like a blanket.

Cigarettes, coffee, and leather.

I was grateful for the cover because I thought I might start shivering to death after the heat had gone away.

"Here's my hoodie," he said and stepped back to look me over, "which you make look a hundred times better than I do." Already, a newfound wave of desire washed over me.

"Doubt that." I snorted and rolled my eyes, but adjusted it until I wore it comfortably.

"And here is a gift—a souvenir from my travels today." He held out a keychain. It was a thin plastic oval, that had a black wolf on it and a white "W" over the front of it.

I couldn't stop the smile that spread over my face.

"The 'W' is for Wolf, I'm assuming." I pointed out as I took it from him and ran my fingers over it.

He nodded slightly.

"I didn't catch the diamond encrusted 'W' on the knife until I got into the house on Saturday."

He smirked at me and ran his hands up and down the outside of my thighs. "A-Are you okay? Is what we just did okay?"

Hearing Jackson stutter almost caused me to fall off the bench. Was he…nervous? Insecure that I didn't like it? Either way, I decided not to give him the satisfaction of my answer, not when he's looking at me with dried blood on his face.

"Are you okay?" I asked and lifted my finger to prod at his busted lip. "What the hell happened?"

I could tell his eyes began to slip back into that work mentality and he started to pull away from me, but I caught his chin and I pulled him back in.

Back to me.

"I'm okay, Olivia. Sometimes when I go to my out-of-town jobs, the old-heads that I deal with don't respect me and my stripes even though I earned them. A lot of them are angry that I outrank them. Sometimes I have to let people know why exactly I'm in the position I'm in." The muscle in his jaw flexed as his eyes found the small candle light.

"Respect? Looks like you got your ass kicked." I challenged.

His gaze bounced back to mine and he leaned in to me close.

"Well, the other guy is no longer breathing, so you tell me who's ass got kicked."

My heart skipped, a small tick of fear running through my logical mind, as excitement danced in his eyes.

He had just left from murdering someone?

Jackson raised his brow and tried to fight the smile that spread over his face. He stepped back and when he began to... adjust himself, I felt the urge to look away.

So, I did.

I jumped down from the bench and was surprised to find that I also had to adjust my sweats, not familiar at all with the sticky feeling between my legs.

"I'm sorry for attacking you when I got here," Jackson said with that deep, demanding, Jackson voice of his, still turned away from me. "My line of work requires me to be a ruthless man, and...you seem to be the only thing that keeps the bad shit away. I got back into town and didn't even stop at home to change or shower…I came here as quick as I could. I had to see you, and when I saw you…" Jackson trailed off, sending a legion of winged beasts flapping through my stomach. "The only thing that I could think was how fucking happy I was that I didn't let that Mack truck turn you into an asphalt pancake."

Despite the serious conversation, his admission practically turns me inside out. To know that I'm an oasis in his desert felt…otherworldly. I wondered if I should tell him that he's the only thing that takes my pain away, even if it's for a little while.

"I'll be your oasis if you'll be mine." I said, hoping that my racing heart wouldn't drown out his response. The keychain clutched in my hand began to make my palms sweaty.

Jackson stayed quiet as he leaned down to pick up his backpack and slung it over his shoulders.

"You're spending your Thanksgiving with your mother and grandmother?" He asked, and finally turned to me.

"Yep, and Sadie always spends it with us." He nodded and opened his mouth to speak but I beat him to it. "What about you? Are you spending it with your family?"

Shadows passed distantly in his eyes and he shook his head softly. "I'm dead to any of those that are still alive."

I scoffed to try to snuff out the sorrow I felt for him. No family. A familiar feeling. "The only thing that matters in this life is the people we love, and those that love us. Don't waste your time. We only get so much of it."

Jackson turned to face me and regarded me silently, and softly, studying my features the way he did in the car on Halloween.

A look that was so much deeper than just a look, just like the first time we locked eyes.

An understanding.

A bond.

He lifted his hand and stroked my jaw with his knuckles. "I have to fly out in the morning, but I'll be home Friday morning." Something in me deflated. "Let me cook you dinner Friday night? My place?"

If those damn butterflies could kill me, I'd be dead and in the ground.

"Okay." I agreed too quickly, too eager to see him again and he hadn't even left yet.

"Okay." He smiled, pressing the pad of his thumb to my lips. "Prepare to have your mind blown with my skills."

"Yes, Chef." I mumbled underneath his touch. He pulled his hand away and kissed me softly, our lips falling into a sweet rhythm together, and he pulled away too quickly.

"Have a good Thanksgiving, I'll see you on Friday." He whispered when he broke away, and he closed in on me to place another kiss to my neck, right below my ear.

"Is there a way that I can get a hold of you? What if I need you?" My feeble attempt at asking for his number made me roll my eyes.

"Oh, baby. You don't need anyone." Jackson smirked and pressed a kiss to my lips once more. My reluctance to his statement doesn't mean it wasn't—and isn't—true.

He backed away from me, fishing his cigarette pack out of his pocket. He pulled one out, ran it between his lips, and lit it up.

And he exited the gazebo without a word, leaving me to blow out the candles, the crunch of the leaves beneath his boots fading away. I stayed for a few moments after he disappeared, waiting to see if I could hear his car engine hum to life, but it never came.

I bent down to collect my coffee mugs and to toss out the hot chocolate, and I realized that he didn't pick up his books that he gifted me. I collected it all anyways and made the small trek back to my house, quietly entering and ascending into my room.

I set everything down on my desk, kept his hoodie on, pulled my sweats off, and collapsed onto my bed with a larger-than-life smile. He hadn't been away from me for ten minutes yet and I was already wondering what he was doing.

Probably showering.

I thought about his busted lip and eyebrow.

I thought about the blood that I tasted when he first kissed me. Jackson's blood.

I thought about when he pulled my shirt off.

And then I thought about how hot it still made me to remember the look on his face when he saw me shirtless.

And as if on cue, my phone vibrated on my nightstand. I rolled over to retrieve it and read a message from an unknown number.

> UNKNOWN: By the way, it's called a gift for a reason. You're not supposed to give it back when you're done. The books were mine, now they are yours.

I smiled like an idiot at my phone, grateful that he gave me what I wanted. My fingers worked to type a quick text back.

> ME: They were beautiful. I'll let you know my thoughts when I see you on Friday. I was a little preoccupied tonight.

My fingers hovered above the keyboard as I waited to see the response bubbles pop up, and they did, but then went away for a few moments. I chewed on my lip nervously until a message comes back through.

> UNKNOWN: I'll listen to any of the thoughts that you want to share with me, for as long as you'll let me.

> UNKNOWN: Get some rest, enjoy spending the holiday with your mother. Somebody wise told me recently that I shouldn't waste my time with people that I love, because we only get so much of it. Happy Thanksgiving, Olivia Charlotte Hayes.

I read the double messages and fully felt my fluttering heart with every word that I read.

There was still a very small and dark whisper in the shadows of my head reminding me that Jackson Wolf, as tall, dark, and handsome as he may be, comes with just as many awful components.

He had *said that he just came from murdering someone.*

Those most basic innate survival skills that kicked in when we first met still rang true in the fact that I should be staying away from him to continue on my life course and become the woman that I want to be. I knew the warning signs when I was near him, and I knew them even away from him.

The only difference between when I first met him, and now, is that those warning bells are a lot quieter. Especially after I've experienced the contentment, and the joy, and the lust, and no amount of warning bells or alarms would be able to stop me from replaying last night over and over and over again until Sadie arrives for Thanksgiving today.

CHAPTER

Nineteen

I head straight to the coffee pot with my head down.

"Oh, look who's back from the dead. Nice of you to join us!" Sadie giggles and I can hear my mother's laughter join her. My hands work to make my coffee.

Nana stays quiet, peeling potatoes in the sink. The coffee pot is only a few feet away from her, and she's the only one not giving me hell, so I decide that she's the one I'll acknowledge first.

"Happy Thanksgiving, Nana." I say and bring my mug to my lips, sipping from the piping hot liquid.

Nana turns to me and look at me over her glasses, "And Happy Thanksgiving to you, my dear." She turns back to the sink.

"Good morning to everyone else in attendance," I say as I turn towards them.

Sadie smiles at me sweetly as she peels the apples. My mother has a suspicious look in her eyes, pausing her task of chopping pecans.

My mother's appearance takes me by surprise. She looks worse than she did yesterday. Her skin is a little more yellow and her eyes a little duller.

"Sadie, has Lottie started smoking cigarettes?" My mother's question, right out the gate, almost topples me over. I find Sadie as soon as her head snaps up to mine, confusion written all over her face.

"Not that I'm aware of." She shakes her head and scrunches her eyebrows at me.

My mother purses her lips. "That's funny. I just caught a whiff of cigarettes when she passed us. Cigarettes and…" she breathes in deep with her eyes closed. "A delicious man."

Out of my peripheral, I can see Nana turn her head to me for just a moment, and then she returns back to her potatoes.

I sip from my mug again, with a soft shake of my head. "I see you still like to make up stories."

My mother scoffs. "Honey, since I've gotten cancer, I've had the most amazing sense of smell. It's comparable to when I was pregnant. What I smell is no story."

Nana turns her head to me again, looking at me expectedly.

"This hoodie was Landon's." I shrug, taking another sip.

"Ha!" Sadie bursts, tossing her head back. "Landon wouldn't touch a cigarette with a ten-foot pole."

"Yeah, you'd know, wouldn't you?" I bite back at her. Sadie clamps her mouth shut.

"Lottie!" Nana scolds, wiping her hands on her apron.

I sigh, my head falling back.

"I only know one person that smokes cigarettes, and it's certainly not Sam Gilbert." Sadie presses further in, and in an instant, my blood pressure is through the roof.

"I haven't been awake for ten minutes and y'all are attacking me." I say dully, taking another sip of my coffee and taking up my spot in the stool on the side of the island, next to Sadie.

"Who's Sam Gilbert?" My mother asks.

"Somebody Olivia met on Halloween. He took her for a ride in his fast car." Sadie grins.

I lean on my elbows, propping my chin up. "He's literally nobody. I haven't even talked to him since then."

"Well, if you're spending time with somebody that smells like that," My mother says mischievously, pointing her knife at me, "Then I can imagine why."

"Is it Jackson?" Sadie asks, pausing mid peel.

"What?" I answer too quickly.

"Oooh," My mother chimes. "Jackson sounds delectable."

"Jackson is the only person that I know that smokes cigarettes. Among other things." Sadie leans into my mother and tells her matter-of-factly.

"You smoke other things, too, Sadie, so don't act like a saint and judge people that you don't know!" I snap at her, my hand out in front of me for effect.

But she only giggles, with a knowing look in her eye. Nana begins working in the sink again, removing all the potatoes from the bay and ridding of the skins.

"It's Jackson. Mr. Tall, Dark, and The-Hottest-Guy-I've-Ever-Seen." Sadie leans into my mother again, telling her information that she doesn't need to know.

A groan tumbles out of me and I palm my face, hoping that this conversation would go any other way besides this way. I wish that Sadie wasn't here when I got Jackson's first book, and I should have never told her about the Connor's visit.

"It's no one, actually, maybe this is just what I smell like." I suggest and lean forward to grab an apple slice, popping it in my mouth.

"Well, the hickey on your neck might suggest otherwise, Lottie." My mother looks to me out of the corner of her eye, and I can hear Nana choke.

"What?!" I stand, my stool scraping across the tile. My hands flying to my throat. Sadie bursts out laughing, practically squealing with joy, and my mind begins racing back to last night—for the millionth time since it's happened.

Jackson *did* kiss me there, but I didn't think it was hard enough to leave a mark.

Oh, God. So embarrassing!

I can feel the heat flood my face. I'd love to bury myself in a hole now and never be seen again.

Except…maybe by Jackson. But first, I'll have to kick his ass for leaving a fucking hickey on my neck!

"Oh, Mama, do you remember the first time you saw a hickey on me?" My mother sighs and smiles giddily. "It feels just like yesterday. I'm so glad I get to experience this before I go." Her voice turns solemn and…there goes the moment, turned into another moment.

"Allison…" Nana says softly, rounding the island to embrace her.

"I tried to hide it from her too, Lottie. Don't worry." My mother reaches up and pats Nana's arms around her. Nana kisses my mother's head and leaves us in the kitchen.

Most likely needing a moment after my mother's shitty comment. She maybe has come to terms about dying, but I don't think that the rest of us are ready to accept it yet.

"So, what's he like?" My mother asks, and Sadie stays quiet. Probably for the first time in her life.

A deep breath fills my lungs as I sit back down in the stool, reaching for another apple slice and a couple pecans.

"He's a criminal." I say plainly. Since everything is getting put on the table.

My mother tilts her head with raised brows. Sadie gives a little giggle.

"A criminal? I think that's an understatement, Liv." Sadie points out, scooping all the peels into a pile so she can begin on the next set of apples.

I sigh defeatedly, knowing that my mother won't let this go, especially since Sadie said *that*.

"The only thing that matters, Mom, is that he is kind to me, and he makes me feel like I'm not alone in this shitty world." I say sternly, trying to give the impression that I don't want to say anything else about it. Jackson is a private man; I don't want him to feel like I've gone and had pillow talk with my mother of all people.

My mother only pays attention to her pecans, chopping them slowly. Her smile is soft, and distant.

"Your father made me feel that way."

What the fuck did she just say to me?

"What?"

She blinks a few times and opens her mouth but nothing comes out.

My mother has always told me that she has no idea who my father is. That she had so many men and lovers that it could be literally anyone.

And now she...she...

"Your father made me feel like I was the only girl in the world. It was a love so strong that it could make magic. Hell, it made you."

My chest rises and falls quickly.

Did I hear her right?

My father?

"Mom..." I say, taking a pause to breathe. "You always said that you didn't know who my father was."

She gives me one nod, but doesn't meet my eye. I look to Sadie and she keeps her head down, tending to her fucking apples.

"I told you that so you wouldn't go looking for him. Your father is…" She trails off, looking for the words.

"He's what?"

"He's a very…powerful man."

The words don't even compute in my brain. I shake my head in disbelief.

"This whole time…" My voice is almost a whisper.

"Lottie, I know you're upset, but—"

"No, I'm not upset, Mom. I—I…I'm angry. I've been dealing with you being the worst mother in the history of mothers and I've had a *father* that I could have been with? I've been lied to my entire life!"

"Please listen to me, Lottie, I—"

"Why should I? How do I know you won't lie to me now?" I try to keep my voice down so I don't disturb Nana wherever she is.

"Because you're finally eighteen. Because I'm dying. And because I have no reason to lie anymore." The old tone of voice that I'm accustomed to hearing from my mother begins to show itself and a sort of anxiety starts to rattle me.

"Mom." I say as plainly as I can, and she finally looks at me. "I have the right to know who my father is."

She chews on the inside of her lip and sets her knife down, brushing her hands over the counter to rid them of pecan crumbs.

Sadie finishes peeling the apple she's on and then follows suit, reaching over to wipe her hands on the hand towel in the center of the island.

My mother crosses one arm over her chest and takes her coffee cup into the other. She leans back in her chair and takes a sip.

"This story isn't just about your father, Lottie, so please… please bear with me and try to listen to everything I say before saying anything or having a thought."

She waits on my response, but I only nod and reach up, finding a lock of hair to twirl around my fingers anxiously.

"When I was seventeen, my best friend's name was Remi," she begins and looks off to the side, at nothing in particular.

"Remi's family was extremely well off, and I lived a life a lot like yours; Daddy died when I was about ten, and this town was suffocating me. One summer, I snuck off with her and her family when they went to vacation for a week at their home in New York. I thought that it was a chance to see the world and meet new people and have the experience of a lifetime."

My mother has never, never took the time to tell me anything about her life. She's never wanted to bond with me in that way, so hearing her speak about herself in her childhood is…almost unreal. The woman that is speaking to me now might as well be another woman completely than the one that I grew up with.

"We arrived and got settled in and we spent a night in downtown Manhattan. There was this fancy restaurant that we ate at and even the wait staff was black tie. It was intimidating. There I was, a country bumpkin girl, in this upscale restaurant. I had no table manners, and I completely made a mess on the only dress that I had. It might as well have been rags."

I'm on the edge of my seat, eating up each word she has to tell me.

I'm finally getting to know something about my father. A story and a person that I've been trying to imagine my entire life.

"I made a mess on myself, I'd spilt soup or a drink or something, and I ran to the bathroom to clean up." My mother smiles as she closes her eyes. "And we ran right into each other."

She sips her coffee. Sadie leans on her propped-up arm and listens as intently as I.

"It was…love at first sight, I think. We just clicked, that moment that we saw each other. He was wearing this gorgeous tux and he had this short dark hair and he just…emanated power. I knew he was somebody. We got lost on the town that night, I ditched Remi and her family and he ditched his. His family is a massive corporate powerhouse and he had just become head of it, picked over his twin brother."

"What's his name?" I ask before she can say anything else.

"Frankie." She smiles, but then corrects herself. "Frank. His brother is Michael. Frank and Michael DeLuca."

I nod, taking in the information, committing it to memory.

Frank DeLuca. My father. With dark hair. Like mine.

"What does he look like?"

My mother smiles again solemnly. "Now? I'm sure age has caught up to him, just as the rest of us, but then?" She sighs and blinks a couple times. "He had the dark hair, and these perfect lips, and his eyes are the same color as yours, that beautiful bright golden hazel. Every time I look at you, I see him."

So then why did she hate me growing up? She talks about him as if he hung the moon but she treated me like I was the complete opposite of their love. Like I was the one who undid it. It doesn't make sense to me.

"Was he kind?"

She nods. "He was. And caring. He had a massive heart. It was Michael who was cruel. The whole of the DeLuca family was powerful and they were all…dangerous. But Michael…"

A chill rocked through her. "Michael was cut from a different cloth. He might as well have been from different blood."

Frank, father, good. Michael, uncle, bad.

All of this information and one question remains unanswered.

"So…" I begin, my heart rate picking up as I even think about saying the words. "I-If you loved my father so much—I mean, you are talking about him like he's your sun, moon, and stars—why aren't you with him? And more importantly, why did I grow up the way that I did with the shittiest mother in the world?"

Sadie's head swings my way with wide eyes, but I don't look at her. I stand my ground with my mother. She only gazes at me, accepting it rather than reacting to it. A sort of satisfaction simmers in a deep and dark part of me as I watch her hold back her response.

She finally levels her eyes with mine and clears her throat.

"Frank and Michael are twins. And so was their father, and their father's father, and their father's father's father, and so on; an age old, long line of twins. The head of the DeLuca family sits in that position for forty years, they get sort of…initiated, when they are twenty-five years old." Still…not answering my question, but I'll bite.

"There can only be one leader, though. How does that work? Does the present leader pick whichever twin he wants?" I interrupt her, wanting to make sure that I understand before she says anything else.

"No. Each set of twins has three 'trials' to undergo." She raises her hands to curl her first two fingers in air quotes.

"Trials…" I shake my head, not quite understanding, and hoping that she expands on it.

"Each present leader uses three variables when deciding who is the successor. This has some kind of guidelines so that fathers aren't picking their favorite son if they don't really qualify." My mother sips her coffee and clears her throat. "The first and most obvious comparison is grade school. Which twin had the best grades, attendance, and character throughout all of school? Throughout the generations, there's almost always one brother that stands out the most. The second test is who had the best scores at some branch of the military. Each set of twins are allowed to decide which branch they'd like to enlist in together, but they must go to the same branch to be graded correctly. The third is that they must do and provide proof of doing an act of love and show of selfishness. Once their evidence is presented, the father will pick which one was a better act of love and show of selfishness. Best two out of three is sworn as the next leader on their twenty-fifth birthday. In case of death, the second in line twin will assume the role."

"This is a hell of a lot of detailed information about a family that you acted like didn't exist," I point out, and continue. "And besides, how does any of that have to do with why you were a shitty mother."

"You have to know the history before you know how it affects you, Lottie." My mother says, which doesn't sound too unreasonable. I should know what my lineage is. I take a shallow breath to calm my nerves and grab my mug to sip from it.

Sadie listens with undivided attention.

"Frankie had just been selected by his father as the new leader when I'd met him, and Michael…he was…" My mother shakes her head, looking for the words as if they are written on the kitchen cabinets. "Michael always believed that he should be alpha. The only thing he was better at though is his performance in the military. They both opted to enlist in the NAVY and train to be NAVY seals. They did one tour and were honorably discharged, returning home to the family business."

"Did you ever meet Michael?" I ask. I'm not sure why that detail is necessary for me to know, but I feel like it matters.

She nods. "I did." She blinks a few times, seemingly remembering long forgotten things. "He's night and day different from Frankie."

"Now, onto answering your question." She says, bracing herself. "That week I spent every waking moment with him. Remi's parents didn't even notice and Remi had found her own man, so I didn't think it was a big deal. I came back home after that week and I found out a month later that I was pregnant. I wrote to him, I told him the news, and a few days later, he was knocking on the door. We'd agreed that the best place for me was right here in Chiefland, because if Michael had known that I was pregnant, he probably would have killed me."

My brows bunch together, why would he have wanted to kill my mo—

"To get rid of any chance of a successor. He wanted to be the leader, but Frankie was the most protected man in the world, Mikey couldn't have taken a shot at him personally. The only other option would have been to take away the person carrying the successors."

Sadie's wide eyes find mine when my mother takes a break to sip from her mug.

"This is like something from a movie, Liv, I can't believe what I'm hearing right now!"

Her excited words are nothing but a whisper as several factors run back through my mind.

My mother stands from her seat, slowly, and collects the pecans, placing them all in a small metal bowl for Nana, and then begins to take care of the finished apples for Sadie.

"I can help you, Ms. Allison." Sadie chimes and stands to help, but I'm practically frozen.

I want to mull over the fact that my mother called my uncle Mikey. Were they all close enough to call each other nicknames? She only spent a week with them. Why was she so close to know all of this information and why is everything so different now?

But all of that sort of fades away as I watch my mother's movements and one single word repeats in my head.

Successor*s*.

As in, plural.

And I remember the very first thing that my mother said when she began telling me the story.

"Frank and Michael are twins. And so was their father, and their father's father, and their father's father's father, and so on; an age old, long line of twins."

Again, the word rattles through me.

Successors.

Not. Just. Me.

If my assumption is correct, I think that I might just pass out.

"Mom…" I began, standing to my feet slowly. She turns from her spot at the sink, rinsing the apples off. Sadie rounds the island again, taking her residence back up on her stool, crossing her arms and bearing her weight on them. "There's another one?"

My mother pauses slightly, her elbows resting on the edge of the sink. She reaches up and twists the knob to turn the water off.

I can see Sadie's head bouncing between us in my periphery.

"His name is Oliver Chase." She says, her back still to me. My knees threaten to buckle beneath me but I stand my ground. My blood whooshes in my ears, echoing my thumping heart.

I have a brother?

All this time I didn't have to suffer alone?

"W-Wh—" I begin to say something, anything, but she cuts me off.

"Lottie, please let me—"

"You tell me the rest of the story, right now, Mom! Why did you make my life hell when you could have had the life of pie?! When we could have lived so much better and happier!"

My mother's cheeks get a tint of pink and tears brim her eyes, her hands flat against the counter.

"There's never been a female DeLuca—one that was *born* into the line. There's never been a woman to lead the family. We knew that Michael would try to kill you, so I hid here until it was time for you and your brother to be born. I kept you, and you father took Oliver. And I-I..." She pauses, takes a deep breath, and looks at me, watery eyes to watery eyes.

"I resented you, because you were the only memory that I had of him, and of what could have been. And he agreed, and he left and never looked back—for your protection—and it *hurt*, Lottie. It almost killed me, baby."

I shake my head in disbelieve, completely in shock.

She knew my father.

She *loved* my father.

Frank DeLuca. All powerful. And dangerous.

I had—have—a brother.

She hated me because I reminded her of a time in her life when she could have had everything. And she had nothing because she kept me.

"So, you decided that it would be easier to hate me, and put me through all this crazy ass psycho shit that I went through, because your feelings were hurt that my father did exactly what you guys agreed to do. That makes a lot of sense, *Mother*."

Her shoulders slump in defeat as she takes my venom.

"Lottie, I was mean to you, and I—"

"'Mean' is a gross understatement." I point out.

My mother takes a deep breath and continues. "I hated myself for it, and it was a vicious cycle of hating myself and resenting you because of everything that I'd lost and didn't have. You were the one reminder that my life wasn't supposed to turn out the way that it did. It's hard to explain. I know you don't understand, bu—"

"No," I stop her, raising my hand in the air for her to stop. "*You* are the one who doesn't understand. You grew up without a father, too, but Nana was *good* to you. You should have been good to me!"

"I know, baby, I tried my best at ev—"

"Screw you!" I scoff. "You tried your best when you tried to kill us both? You tried your best when four dudes rape you in front of me? You tried your best when your seventeenth boyfriend asked me, at the ripe old age of twelve, if I could flash him? You didn't try shit, and I can't believe you're dropping this, this *nuclear bomb* on me as if I'm just supposed to be okay with the fact that I've gone my entire life not knowing my father and brother, when I could have been around them this whole time. I'm absolutely..." My words fall short when emotion clogs my throat.

Sadie sits there and scrolls through her phone. At some point she'd pulled it out of her pocket, and I'm sure only to seem like she wasn't infringing on our conversation.

"I made awful choices, but I did the best that I could with what I had." She tries a shitty defense, but it just stokes those coals that are blazing bright.

"Well, your best wasn't good enough, Mom! You were a junkie and an alcoholic and a stripper. 'Your best' means shit to me. You were a *bitch* for the entirety of my life, and I'm all fucked up in the head now because of your selfishness. You should have just let Michael do what he wanted to do. He would have saved you all this trouble." I swallow down the lump in my throat and sit back down, a few deep breaths coming in and going out.

We both sit here in silence, mulling over the facts that were just presented to me. My harsh words seem to roll of her shoulders quicker than water off a duck's feathers.

"I love you, Lottie, and I'm here to make things right in whatever capacity I can." She turns her head to me, and clears her throat. Her hands reach up to blot her cheeks.

"I'm going to check on Nana, and then I think I'm going to take a rest. I'm pretty tired after chopping up all those pecans. I'll see you a little later." She says, and as she exits the room, my heart begins to twist and turn in every way possible and for every reason imaginable.

I'm absolutely floored. Every single cell in my body, every nerve, every ounce of common sense is telling me to hate her forever. How could she keep something like this from me? I've been living a lie for my entire life.

Olivia Charlotte DeLuca. That's what my name would have been. My twin brother. Oliver Chase DeLuca.

My father. My father who has dark hair and golden eyes like me. This whole time I've had a family. A family that wouldn't have required me to live this bullshit life that I've lived.

This whole time I thought that I was alone.

I'm so angry at her, I'm so enraged with my mother that I can practically feel the arteries bulging out of my neck. I just cannot believe that she would keep something like this from me. And that she would blame *me* for her life turning out this way!

I didn't ask to be born! I didn't ask for any of this, she could have aborted me—us!

A small movement from Sadie catches my attention and I blink once, clearing all thoughts from my mind. All the hatred. All the anger. All the confusion and the loneliness and the disbelief and the complete *sadness*. I push it out of my mind and I look to my best friend.

"Tell me what you're thinking right now, Sadie."

She looks at me with her crystal blues and she pulls her bottom lip between her teeth.

"Oh, Liv…I don't even know what to say."

"Tell me exactly what you're thinking." I demand, trying to keep my head clear until I get a third point of view.

"I think that you just had a grenade thrown at you and you had no cover to take. I think that your life just got, quite literally, blown to smithereens, and you have every right to be upset with her. I know the life that you lived when you were younger. I know what you went through, and I can understand why you would never want to talk to her again. She robbed you of the life you were supposed to live." Sadie leans forward on her stool and reaches out to grab my left hand.

"But…" She continues, "I also think that you, just as well as I do, know that life is far too short. I think that your mother is extremely sick, and it's a miracle that she's here today, and that she had the ability to tell you all of this stuff about yourself and your family. I think that's important. I think that you need to push all of that 'could'a, should'a, would'a' out of your mind and focus on the most important thing here: she's trying to make amends for all the stuff that she admittedly did. She knows she was a bad mom. She hurts from it. She has cancer, an aggressive one that will claim her soon, and I bet you, that all she's hoping to die with is your forgiveness."

Sadie's words bring a memory to the forefront of my mind. The one on my fourth birthday when we were sitting on the bench.

"All of this that we are dealing with, all of this bullshit, is to keep you safe, Lottie. One day, one day you will realize that. I'm sorry that I'm a horrible mother. Your father wanted better for you."

The day has finally come; she made good on her promise to tell me how she ended up this way. I've never had my heart broken to where I wanted to turn to drugs and alcohol to take it all away, and I hope that I never have to.

And now it's all out on the table. I know everything now. I'm no longer in the dark about my life and my family and their history. I do have a strong wonder about him, my father. I'd love to meet him. I'd love to meet my brother even more.

That urge, though, that urge is why she didn't tell me. She'd knew that I'd want to find them and meet them, and keeping it this way, Oliver will be the one to assume the head of the DeLuca family when it's time, and Michael won't have a chance to remove me from the equation.

Knowing all that, and I still have this innate urge to meet them, no matter how cruel they might be.

"I just can't believe that she's kept something this big from me this whole time. I thought that I knew what it felt like to be in the dark with you and Landon, and yet…this is exponentially worse."

Sadie nods thoughtfully, her chin resting in her palm.

"Liv," she begins, squeezing my hand, "before anyone else at school, you were suffering. You've been handling this kind of pain for our entire lives, like an absolute queen, and I think that says something. Not everyone is equipped to carry the burden you've carried, and still, here you are. Still alive, still standing.

Tall. Taller than any of us peons." Her words are kind, moving me slightly on my position and my feelings. "Forgiving your mom wouldn't be for her to die peacefully knowing you forgave her. It would be for you to live peacefully, despite knowing all the bad things. Forgiveness is love, Olivia. Don't let her die thinking that you still and will always hate her, because one day when you're fully ready to let that weight go…she won't be here to accept it from you." Tears brim her blue eyes, and I know it in my bones that she's right.

Jackson's last text comes to mind, I can almost see the blue chat bubble.

"Get some rest, enjoy spending the holiday with your mother. Somebody wise told me recently that I shouldn't waste my time with people that I love, because we only get so much of it."

I had said that to him. I was the wise person to give Jackson that advice, and I was thinking of all the time that I wouldn't get with Landon when I'd said it.

Wouldn't it make sense to practice what I preach?

I do love her; I love her stupidly. She's my mother, why wouldn't I? My entire eighteen years have gone by for this day, to know everything.

And here it is.

Nana appears around the corner from the laundry room door, her face holding a notion of joy.

Until she sees me and the look on my face.

"What happened?" She asks, looking between Sadie and I.

"Did you know?" I ask her.

"Did I know what?"

"About me. About Frank and Oliver DeLuca. About the fact that my mother lied to me for my entire life?"

Nana shifts her weight uncomfortably and starts heading to the sink.

"Lottie..." She says, almost warningly.

"Did you know, Nana?" I ask again, but this time, a lot softer and a little resigned.

Her shoulders deflate and she turns to look at me.

"I did. It was only for your protection." She says with no more defense.

I nod my head, "I know."

"I'd do it all again. A beautiful lady like you has no business running an...organization like theirs. You are going to school to do whatever you want to do, Lottie. You don't need their last name to make your way." She approaches me and touches my cheek softly, smiling in that sweet way of hers.

"I know, Nana. I'm not upset." I respond, covering her hand with mine.

"You're not?" Confusion crosses her features.

"Well..." I look to Sadie. "I definitely was at first." She cracks a smile and I look back at Nana. "But I think it would be the adult thing of me to forgive her, and try to salvage what is left of this Thanksgiving." I say, the words constricting my throat.

Nana's eyes water and she smiles lovingly. "My sweet grandbaby, who has a heart way too big for this family. I love you." She pulls me into a hug and I squeeze her tightly.

"I love you, too, Nana."

"Now," She begins and pulls away just enough to look at me, "Just because you're grown, now, doesn't mean that you can go around getting into fights with vacuums and vampires." And her eyes drop to my neck. Sadie giggles next to us.

Embarrassment floods my cheeks and I nod in agreement. "You're absolutely right, Nana, but this particular vacuum just...malfunctioned and I couldn't help it." Sadie giggles again, and I try to stifle my own laugh. "It must have been operator malfunction so I'll try to control it better next time."

"Oh, there's going to be a next time?" Sadie raises her brows and a smirk sits on her perfect lips.

I shrug. "Maybe, maybe not. I guess we will see."

Nana claims that she's heard enough and begins delegating our next tasks, only having a few more hours until supper time. We begin piecing together the last dishes, and I wait patiently for my mother to take her rest, having the strangest feeling that things might be different between us when she wakes.

It's tradition in the Hayes family to go around the table at Thanksgiving and each person say what they are thankful for.

Nana finished all of the food up just in time for sunset, and the pies are still in the oven, going to be hot and ready when we are finished eating.

So here we are, with mountainous plates and smiles from ear to ear.

"I'll start this year!" Sadie pipes up and we all wait for her to start. She swallows once, looking at the food on her plate. "I'm thankful for what this year has given, and taken away. I've experienced love in all capacities, and I'm super grateful to have had the chance. Okay, next person." She says with a glisten in her eyes.

"I'm grateful," Nana begins as she sets her fork down and clasps her hands in her lap. "For the chance to see my baby for this amazing holiday, and to know that she is exactly where she needs to be in life. I don't know why God inflicted you with this sickness, baby, but I know that it's brought you home to me, and that's all that matters." Nana reaches out to grab my mother's hand and they share a solemn look.

"I'm grateful for the cancer." She says with tears in her eyes. At first, I feel repulsed. Why would she be grateful for dying? "It brought me back home; it made me realize just how short life is and how much I regret spending it the way that I did. I'm grateful for my amazing mother and my out-of-this-world baby girl. You've grown into such an incredible woman and I couldn't be any prouder than I am right now. I know that whatever you do in this life, you will excel at, and you will help change lives, and liberate young girls, and be an extraordinary woman. I love you, Olivia Charlotte. Happy Thanksgiving, y'all."

My mother's words bring tears to my eyes for the millionth time in my life, but this time, it's for a different reason entirely.

For the first time in my life, my mother looks me in the eyes and I see her for the woman that she is.

The real one.

For the first time, I feel like she sees *me*.

An understanding between us, as mother and daughter. It clicks into place. I do love her, the woman that gave me life. She didn't have much to do with nurturing as I grew, but all it took was a few sentences at Thanksgiving dinner for that part of me to lift off my chest.

For my resentment to disappear.

"This year...I am thankful for the time that I had with my friend, Landon. I miss him dearly," My throat tries to close up but I swallow it down and continue. "But I am very glad that he no longer has to live the life that he'd started to live. I'm thankful for my friend, Sadie, and the way she's here for me after all of this. I'm thankful for my Nana for everything that she's done for me. And finally," I say, bracing myself and wiping my palms on my jeans. "I'm thankful for this time with my mother, this time to heal and this time to learn who I am and where I come from. I'm thankful for the fact that I'm seeing the bigger picture, and understand and don't feel the need to hold any hate or contempt in my heart towards the situation, and I'm thankful that I get to feel it before it's too late. And finally, I'm thankful for this incredible dinner that we all made." I end with a smile on my face and a warmth in my chest. A few sniffles reach me as I look around to my family and friend, watching them wipe away their tears.

"Anyways, let's eat, please!" I say with a nervous laugh and pick my silverware up. From there, we eat, we drink, and we laugh until we can't breathe anymore. This family dinner is one that I've been waiting for my entire life, as whole as it could be at the moment.

I wish that I could get the chance to stay here forever, with this new version of my mother, but even I know, that all things must come to an end.

There won't be an invisible force to save her this time.

CHAPTER

Twenty

"Should I be scared?" I ask Jackson nervously.

I sit in Jackson's passenger seat with my seatbelt on and a blindfold covering my eyes. My knee bounces in anticipation and my hands won't stop sweating.

"Have you ever been scared of me?" He asks darkly, his lips right next to my ear. His breath against the shell of my ear sends chills across my neck and down my arms.

Have I? I've been nervous and unsure at times, but have I ever truly been scared of him? Even in times when I should have, I found myself wanting to push him further.

"That's what I thought." He chuckles and his voice goes farther away. "Just sit back and relax, nobody knows where I live, so this is just a precaution."

Nobody knows where he lives? He did tell me that he doesn't have any family, but what about friends? Is his life really so isolated that *nobody* knows where he lives?

The radio's volume increases and I do what he says, I lean my head back against the seat's headrest and my mind drifts with the melody of whatever oldies rock is playing through the speakers. The music has an unexpected calming effect on my psyche even though I can't see anything.

I trust him. Probably a hell of a lot more than I should.

Brave? Or stupid?

When I woke this morning, my mother had asked me what I was up to for the day, and I lied, telling her that I was going out with Sadie.

I've never gone through the regular teenage act of needing to tell my mother where I was going. I never had to, considering that she was absent, but it felt strange lying to her. She wouldn't have cared if I'd told her I was having dinner with Jackson. I suppose I was trying to avoid a million questions, but lying to her didn't feel right.

I think that I lied to her because I wanted to lie to myself. I've been nervous all day, anticipating tonight. I had no idea what to expect. No idea what to wear. No idea how to act.

He'd said he wanted to make me dinner at his place but... does that mean that he expects sex? I don't think I'm ready for something like that. We've barely just kissed.

An unexpected heat wave has decided to interrupt the holiday chill, so, I opted to wear a pair of khaki shorts, shorter than I usually would go for. Certainly, never something I'd wear to school. I picked through my closet for what seemed like hours before finally deciding on a white, sleeveless blouse that has beautiful orange and pink flowers throughout the fabric. It reminded me of sunsets when I'd first saw it, and I figured it fit the bill.

But I feel so naked.

I showered and shaved—everywhere. I lotioned and conditioned and felt like I was getting prepped for auction. I'm not sure why I felt the need to do all of it, but it felt important for some reason.

Just when I think that my heart might explode from angst, a large, warm hand rests on my thigh.

"Where are you running to, baby?" Jackson's voice paired with his gentle touch sends a different kind of angst through my system, but calming nonetheless.

My knee stops bouncing and I take a deep, stabling breath.

"We're here." He says, his hand falling away from my skin. I feel his fingers at the back of my head, fumbling with the blindfold.

The cover over my eyes falls away and it only takes me a few seconds to realize that we are in a garage. The walls are lined with tools and boxes, just like a regular man in at the age of...

How come I've never thought to ask how old Jackson is? Am I completely and utterly delusional?

Am I falling for a man and I have no idea how old he is? What if he's, like, fifty years old? Am I insane?

I've been completely blinded by his charm and his smile and his eyes that always say more than his mouth does, and—

"Olivia." Jackson's voice pulls me back down to earth and my head snaps to him. "Are you okay?"

I nod my head and but my smile is a bit lackluster. "I've just never..."

"You don't have to stress. We are just having dinner. Relax, baby." He assures me with a soft and knowing smile.

I follow Jackson's lead in stepping out of his car, and follow him through the door leading into his home.

Sure, I know Jackson in his element, from Landon, I know his protective ways even though we've barely known each other. We've been alone numerous times.

But this? Being inside Jackson Wolf's home feels so incredibly intimate. His words play through my mind. *"Nobody knows where I live."*

Seeing something that nobody else has seen makes me feel...massively elated.

"I'll give you a tour later, but for right now, you can follow me. I've got everything pretty much prepped to cook." Jackson says in front of me.

We pass through the laundry room first, and then we step into a short hallway that ends with three different doors. All of the walls are beautifully white, and the floors are wooden and glossy.

Cozy.

As soon as we enter his home, a delicious smell engulfs me, and I know that he's already been here cooking. Has he been anticipating this all day like I have?

"This way," Jackson gestures to his left, "is the bed rooms, there's three. This way," he gestures to our right, "is the guest bathroom and a secondary sitting room, which I have set up as a library. And this way," he gestures before us, "is the kitchen and dining room." His hand lands on the small of my back as he guides me through the doorway to the right of us, sending me into…the library? I can make out a giant case on the wall and what looks to be like books.

"How was your Thanksgiving, Olivia?" Jackson asks, flipping the light switch on the wall. The Victorian-style sconces flicker to life, creating the most serene aura. Three walls are lined from top to bottom, side to side, with book shelves, and utterly full of books.

So many books.

A small cart sits next to the end, right by the door, and it's full of books as well, a pile starting on the floor next to it.

A small black couch, a couple of matching chairs sit around a beautiful marble coffee table, matching end tables sit between the chairs.

On the wall that's not lined with books, is a massive dark wood cabinet, holding all kinds of liquors and wines. Glasses and utensils to make drinks and a small sink are all put in their proper place in the cabinet. All the way at the end sits an ice machine, the soft hum of it becoming recognizable.

Is he like…rich? Look at this place.

"Olivia?"

My head snaps around to him in the midst of doing another once-over and I raise my brows in question.

"How was your Thanksgiving?" He asks me, his shadowy skeleton hand running through his perfectly tousled black hair. Like muscle memory, his hands begin to work to retrieve glasses and liquor from the cabinet, and his eyes never leave mine.

"It was good, actually. I was grateful for a lot of things this year." I take a couple steps closer to him, my hip leaning against the countertop where he continues to make our drinks. He finally looks away as he retrieves an orange, a container of cherries, and some sugar. A bottle of Wild Turkey 101 sits next to the glasses, almost empty.

This must be his favorite one.

"Did you spend time with your mother?" He asks, focused on the task in front of him. Oh, that must be a loaded question.

"I did, after she got a whiff of your scent on your hoodie and noticed the hickey on my neck." I try not to smile, but I can't help it. Especially when he pauses for a moment, looks to me, and then to my neck. His dimple begins to pop out as he fights his own smile and a breathy laugh tumbles out from me.

"You're a consenting adult. I hope she didn't try to give you the Romeo and Juliet speech." He stops working for a moment to listen to my response.

My mouth goes to say that she didn't, but my mind stops me, pushing out the most important thing that she did say. "She actually told me about my father, for the first time."

Jackson's head tilts slightly. "You've never known him?"

I shake my head, clearing my throat. "She's always told me that she never knew who he was, that she was working as a prostitute when she got pregnant with me and she didn't care to find out. She hated me when I was growing up, and never wanted to have much of a conversation." Jackson's eyes thin slightly but then he returns to his task of making our drinks.

"No mother hates her child, truly." Jackson pours some sugar in the bottom of both glasses, and pours a small bit of a liquid that I'm unfamiliar with on top, swirling the glass around to mix the two together. "If she treated you horribly...why did you forgive her so easily?"

I take a deep breath and a moment to think about the question as he retrieves a couple cubes of ice and plops them in the glass.

"I didn't want to, honestly." I say and shake my head. I take another deep breath and he grabs a knife out of one of the drawers, peeling off a piece of the orange. "When she came back, I was relieved to know she was alive, but when I found out about her cancer and that she was inevitably going to die, I wished she'd just stayed away. And yesterday she finally had a heart to heart with me, telling me everything that I've ever wanted to know. It was refreshing to talk to her like a daughter would talk to her mother, she said all the right things, I guess. I got my answers."

"So forgiving. So loyal to the people you love." Jackson murmurs, scooping a cherry from the jar and slipping it into the glass, topping it off with the brown liquid. He caps the bottle and dips his middle finger in, swirling the mixture around twice, and suddenly I'm hyperaware of his fingers, and hands, and the muscles moving and shifting underneath his skeleton-inked skin. In an instant, I'm thrown back to a couple nights ago and just how those same hands felt on my bare skin.

"And what did you find out about your father?" He asks when I don't respond, and raises his finger to his lips, ridding the drink from his skin. I hold my hand out, taking the drink from him, and realize just how dry my mouth is.

I shrug, lifting the glass to my lips, pausing to say the first thing that comes to mind. "That there's no point in chasing shadows."

Jackson watches me closely as I sip the first sip, mimicking my actions. "That's a very mindful statement from someone your age." He tilts his head thoughtfully.

Before I can even comment on the taste of the drink, I respond to his statement. "It's true, nonetheless. She kept him a secret for a reason. There's no point in me sticking my nose where it doesn't belong."

He stays quiet for a few moments, his green eyes studying me.

The Old Fashioned that he prepared is light, and a little zesty, and refreshing. I can, and probably will, at some point, get drunk off of these.

"What are your thoughts on the drink?" He asks.

"It's pretty good. I've had better, though." I say, tilting my glass toward him playfully.

Jackson raises his brows. "Better Old Fashioneds or better drinks?"

"Better drinks."

"Mmm." He hums against his glass. His throat rolls with his swallow and he speaks again, drawing my attention upward to his lips. "Come," he raises his glass toward the door behind me, "I need to tend to the sauce."

Jackson steps around me and I turn to follow, my glass gripped between my fingers.

It's only a few steps before we hit the intersection by the laundry room and turn right into the kitchen.

I never thought that I would be intrigued by a kitchen, but alas, Jackson Wolf never fails to surprise me.

It's absolutely massive. The cabinets are all white with glass panes, the knobs and hinges all gold. The sink fixture and the light fixtures are all gold. My head falls back as I look up, taking in the painted ceiling, as if Michelangelo himself commissioned it. A beautiful small chandelier hangs from the ceiling, but up high enough that a metal grate hangs just over the island, all of the cast iron pots and pans hang from it on hooks.

The island in the middle has a chopping block, and the surrounding counters have the most beautiful marble that I've ever seen: a white base with golden specks and forest green veins spidering all throughout.

Jackson walks directly to the corner of the kitchen where he lifts the lid on the crockpot. He picks up a wooden spoon out of the container next to the stove and stirs the mixture.

"What are you making?" I ask across the kitchen.

He keeps his back to me as he closes the lid and takes a few steps toward the refrigerator.

"I made homemade tomato sauce that's been simmering on low all day, and I have homemade meatballs that I'm going to sear, and I was going to make homemade noodles but I've got a box of store-bought ones that I think I'll use instead." He grabs a container that's covered with aluminum foil and sets it on the counter next to the stove.

"So, you work all night," I begin, leaning against my elbows on the furthest side of the island. "You work all day," I continue, as he sets a pan on the gas stove and turns the knob, the flame coming to life. "And you make food from scratch. Do you ever sleep?"

His motions slow for a moment, but he continues after a second. I watch him grab the container and yank the foil off the top, and then the searing sound of meat hitting the hot pan.

When he stays quiet, I pick up my glass and take a sip, pushing off the chopping block to walk around and join him at the stove.

"It's much easier to be awake than it is to sleep." He says solemnly. His eyes are distant as he pushes around the meatballs, smokey goodness beginning to lift up and fill the kitchen. "The work that I do is…effortless. The lives I've had to take were only a job at the time. It was easy. The hard part is those lives coming for me when I sleep." Jackson stirs the meatballs one more time and turns to retrieve a pot from the hanging rack, and turning back to fill it up at the sink a few steps down the counter.

"What do you mean they come for you when you sleep?" I inquire as I take another sip.

Jackson sets the pot on the stove and turns the knob, another flame blazing. He reaches for his glass and takes a sip.

"I see them. I see their faces before they died, begging me not to take their life. Some of them deserved it, some of them didn't. I see people who I've had to smack around. Ones that I've had to hurt badly. It's all part of the job. And it makes it hard to sleep at night."

He reaches for a bottle of oil above the stove and squirts some in the pot of water, and pushes around the meatballs once more, the smell absolutely beginning to make my mouth water.

I sip from my glass again, realizing that I'll be out in just a few more sips.

"It seems that your shadows are chasing you."

He tilts his head and smiles a soft smile, before gripping the handle of the pan and dumping the meatballs into the sauce off to the side.

"You are clever, Olivia Charlotte Hayes."

I sip the last few sips. "I try to be. And I did say that I've had better drinks, but this is the best damn Old Fashioned I've ever had, and I would love if you'd make me another one, Jackson Wolf."

A carefree laugh tumbles out of him, and it warms my chest in the best way.

That's a laugh meant just for me.

Jackson turns and eyes me playfully, tapping the wooden spoon on the side of the crockpot and setting it on a small plate on the counter.

"I can do that." He steps to me and his index finger and thumb catch my chin, pulling it up to meet his face. "For a kiss."

"I can do that." I whisper back and press my lips against his, savoring the warmth of his skin against mine. He pulls away too quickly and steps around me to retrieve the ingredients from the library.

Jackson disappears behind me and I step over to the sauce, taking the liberty to stir it. My mouth waters again at the smell of the meatballs melding with the tomato sauce.

This is going to be incredible.

I place the lid back on as I hear Jackson's footfalls against the hardwood, and there's one thing that I want to ask him about.

Jackson sets the ingredients on the island and I spin around to place my empty glass in front of him.

"You said that I was forgiving and loyal to the people I love, and it's not the first time you've said something like that. Do you think I shouldn't have? That I should keep letting it fester?" I ask him, leaning on my elbows as I watch him and his hands work thoughtfully.

His eyes focus on his task, and he pulls his bottom lip between his teeth, slowly dragging it through until it's free and he takes a breath.

"The first day that I met you, you threw yourself in front of your friend to protect him when he was in danger. The second time I met you, you had just been humiliated and degraded by that same friend—which was entirely unacceptable and I wanted to break his neck for it, for exposing you to all those people." I listen intently to his words, eating up every syllable. He follows the same routine that he did with the first drink, and I watch him carefully. "Both of your friends betrayed you and yet, you have since forgiven them."

"Well, one of them is dead, so..."

He flashes me a look, those fucking eyes always making my head swim. "But before that. You forgave him so quickly."

"I wallowed in my self-pity for three days before I did, though."

He pours the alcohol into the glass and swirls with his middle finger again, sucking the liquid off just like he did the first time.

"Did you know that they were together?" I ask, a little nervous of the answer.

His hands pause for a moment before he pushes my drink across the wood towards me.

"Yes."

"That's why you gave me shit about being loyal to Landon when you saw me at Connor's."

He tips his glass towards me. "Precisely."

"I miss him." I say solemnly. "Can you tell me about it? About that night, I mean. All I know is what Sadie found out through Ryan."

Jackson sighs and sips from his glass. "Ryan hasn't been initiated, so he only knows what he hears through the grapevine." I raise my glass to my lips, sipping carefully.

I think I'm already feeling the first glass.

He steps around the island and me, to the stove to check the water. It's not quite boiling yet so he leans back against the counter, and runs his hand through his hair.

"Not long ago there was a group of my guys that went rogue. I've not been able to locate them, until my boss got a tip that they were going to hit a Bank of America in a small town in Alabama. My guys, my responsibility. We were supposed to terminate them, confiscate the cash, and come home, everyone home in time to eat steak and potatoes, have a drink, and still get eight hours of sleep."

"It was only the two of you?"

"Yes.

"Against how many guys?"

"Five."

A breath gets punched out of my lungs. Statistically, those aren't good odds. I know Jackson acts like he's big and bad, but there's no way that he could take four people if Landon were to be tied up with only one.

"So, what happened?" I press, remembering how he showed up and stole me away from the Halloween party, and how he told me that Landon was out of state on a bank job. He wasn't robbing a bank, but the job was still just as dangerous.

"Before I say anything else, you should know that I am a massive computer geek."

I make a face at him, despite the serious conversation. "That's fine, but nobody says geek anymore. You have to be at least twenty-five."

A chuckle rumbles through the air between us and it's a sound that scratches a certain itch in my brain.

"Guess my age by the end of the night and I'll give you a prize."

"Oh, you're on. I have a thing for reading people."

"So, I developed an algorithm to send me a notification when your name is sent in any texts or emails or messages on social medias for people in your group. You know, the people closest to you. I got several notifications with your name when we'd just landed the package from them that night. Three of them got away, but we were over the Florida Georgia Line, and were pretty much home free." He is quiet for a moment, as if recalling what happened, and I take the moment to remember how frantic he was when he took me home.

"We split it up, half with him and half with me, and we took different routes back to town, and I hauled ass to get to you, hoping in the name of all things holy that your stupidity didn't get you killed. I'd never heard of this Sam Gilbert, I checked and I cross-checked and—"

"Wait, why do you have that, though?" I interrupt him.

"What do you mean?"

"Why do you have that? Why do you need to know about my safety? I'm just a regular girl from high school, I don't think I'm in any imminent danger, Jackson." I tell him, and try to be as least condescending as possible. I don't want him to feel like he's crazy or demean his actions, but getting notified any time somebody in my "circle" messages another person about me seems a little much.

There's a reason your mother hid you away from your father's family, Olivia.

The small voice raises the hair on my neck, and I don't even want to talk about it anymore.

With Jackson's back to me, he steps to the left from the stove to stir and taste the sauce once more.

"I think that a young woman as breathtaking as you is always in imminent danger." Jackson turns to face me, taking the couple steps between us and he reaches up to tuck my hair behind my ear. "And I've already told you that I fear who I might become if anything were to happen to you."

My skin practically vibrates with the need for his touch.

"You're already as bad as they come, from what I hear. I'd be condemning you to something far worse than hell." I say softly, my hands reaching up to lock behind his neck.

"For you? I'd endure it a thousand times over." He whispers against my lips before capturing them in a kiss that makes my head spin. One that I've been yearning for since he left the night before Thanksgiving.

He pulls my bottom lip between his teeth, slowly letting it slip away from his hold. Jackson's hands roam over my back and down over my ass, scooping behind my thighs to lift me up onto the counter. He never breaks away, his lips and tongue working to take every ounce of breath from my lungs.

It's all becoming his, anyways.

Even when I'm not with him, everything that I do, everything that I say, everything that I see and hear and touch, I think about Jackson in some form. We are two completely different people from different walks of life, and yet, our souls couldn't be more alike.

My mind and my heart is dealing with Landon's death, and already grieving for my mother before she's even passed, and yet, it's all background noise when I'm with him.

I open my knees wide enough for Jackson to stand between them, and it suddenly feels like I'm on fire. His fingertips slide under the hem of my shorts on my thigh and he finally breaks away from me, looking down to his fingers.

Something that I haven't worried about in so long suddenly resurfaces.

My scars.

In an instant, a deep-rooted panic strikes me and I suck in a breath the moment my lips are free. My hands leave his shoulders and fly to my skin to cover the thin white lines. The blood roars in my ears as my heart thumps away.

His hands fall away from my thighs and I cover them with my own. My face is beet red. And hot. So, so hot. Embarrassment floods my mind and clouds my vision.

They are the reason that I wear only long pants. I don't want anyone to see them, ever, and have to explain them.

"Olivia." Jackson's deep and demanding voice rumbles through my frame, but my eyes squeeze shut, frozen with fear.

What is he going to think?

"I'm sorry, Jackson." I say, and lift my hands to push against his chest, but he catches them and holds them out, away from both of us. I finally open my eyes to see his head falls as he inspects those small marks.

I feel so small.

I want to hide.

"What is this from?" He asks me when he pushes the hem of my shorts up higher to reveal more.

"Nothing, really. It was just an accident from a long time ago." My words are rushed and my heart has made no attempt to slow.

"This was no accident. Did you do this to yourself?" His voice is soft, and almost sad, and when he lifts his head to look at me, I swear that I almost collapse.

His eyes are filled with an emotion that I can't quite place, and they are pleading.

But I only shake my head and tears brim my eyes. "I don't want you to see them." I whisper, my fingers trying to tug the shorts to cover the scars. "I've spent so long trying to hide them, I just wish they would disappear."

"Hey," Jackson hums in that soothing, honey-like voice of his, "Look at me. Right here, Olivia, look at me."

I do, wiping the tears from my face. The corners of his lips turn upwards slightly, and he reaches up, tucking my hair behind my ear, and tracing the curve of my jaw. His pointer finger applies the smallest bit of pressure, guiding my back to him, our noses brushing softly.

"There is nothing about yourself that I want you to hide. Absolutely nothing that you reveal to me could change what I feel. And there's especially nothing to apologize for." He says his words intently and deliberately, and I feel them in my soul.

I feel them in a way that I've never felt anything before, way down deep and way out wide, making that panic slowly slip away. A settling breath fills my lungs, and my heart begins to slow.

How silly of me to think that Jackson Wolf would be scared off by a couple scars of all things.

"That's my girl, just breathe. Unless you carve out my heart and burn my remains, nothing, and I mean nothing at all, could force me from you. *Especially* not a couple scars. No matter the reason they are there." He presses a kiss to the top of my head and pulls me into his chest, our midsections flush together.

"Why did you do it?" He asks, but not out of judgement, only curiosity.

"I think that I just got to a time in my life where I wanted to feel something different than the pain that I felt on a daily basis. I wanted control. My mother was horrible in every way. It was so dark inside my mind that I didn't see any light, and I felt so alone all the time. I had Sadie and Landon, but they had families. I didn't. When my mother found out..." I blow out a breath and shake my head. "She tried to kill us both. It was a disaster."

"Your mother tried to kill you both?" Jackson's hands ball up into fists against my thighs. His timbre pours a tension into my shoulders. I didn't ever want him to know this much, to see me and her for what we are.

A couple of crazy, psychotic, messes.

I sigh.

No lying.

"In a car accident. I think she was coming down off of whatever drug of the week she had."

His lips press into a line and he blinks a few times, studying my face in the way that he does.

"Is that the worst thing she's ever done?" He asks, his face hard.

I shrug, trying to downplay what I just revealed. "I've seen some pretty fucked up things when it comes to her. When I was a girl, probably ten or eleven, I walked out to see her getting raped by four guys, right in our living room."

"Olivia, tell me that's not true." He presses, any semblance of humor gone from his features.

"It is. One of the guys held me there and made me watch. And when I was helping her afterwards, like...clean up, she blamed it on me. She's said that if I'd tried harder to stop them, then it wouldn't have happened." I force down the painful memory.

Jackson is quiet for some moments, before he responds; his usual calm and collected demeaner making an appearance. His hands relax and rest against my skin.

"She hurt you tremendously, the woman that was supposed to make sure that no harm comes to you, she hurt you repeatedly, and yet…you've still forgiven her after all these years." He murmurs, pressing a soft kiss to the tip of my nose.

"I did. If she dies—which, she will soon—and I never got the chance to accept what's in the past is exactly that, then I'd never forgive myself." I say, feeling a lot lighter than the beginning of the conversation. The alcohol is probably a huge contributor. "Life is too short."

Jackson slips out of my grasp and turns around to check on the noodles. "Indeed, it is."

I turn at the waist, looking for my drink, and I pick up the glass from behind me, bringing to my lips.

Jackson works quietly as he places a colander in the sink and pours the noodles.

I sip, he works.

My thoughts drift to Landon for a moment. Would he approve of Jackson and I if he knew I was safe? I'd like to think that he would only care about my happiness, regardless of who I found it with.

Jackson retrieves two places from the cabinets above the counter that he's at and he sets them gently on the counter. They are square, and a deep forest green with gold trim. It's so strange to see Jackson's tastes. My mind pictures him as a regular man with basic taste, but his home is beautiful, and clean, and… expensive.

I remember when I thought something similar on Halloween night about his car.

Jackson makes our plates, noodles first and then a couple scoops of the sauce and meatballs.

"Silverware is in that drawer if you don't mind grabbing it." Jackson points to the drawer that's underneath my dangling legs and I hop down, holding my glass in one hand, and grabbing the silverware with the other. Fork, spoon, and knife.

"Can I have another drink, before we sit down?" I ask him sheepishly. Jackson sets the plates back down on the counter and flashes me a grin. It's not as bright as it was before our dull conversation. I hope that I didn't kill the mood.

"I knew you'd like them. But you should slow down, Tito, before I'm carrying you out of here."

A warm feeling spreads over my skin and I feel light and airy. "Whatever," I giggle, and slide my glass to him. He silently prepares my drink, and another one for himself after he downs the rest of the first glass.

"Can you carry my glass for me?" He asks, and I nod, fisting both of them. He took the silverware from me and put them on top of the plates, and he begins to leave the kitchen, rounding the corner to the dining room.

Once again, I'm shocked by the extravagance.

The dining room table is dark, and large, and shiny. It easily seats twenty people. The chairs are the same dark wood, with sewn on mattresses, forest green, of course.

There's a massive China cabinet the size of one entire wall with beautiful dish sets and glasses and plates. The walls are white, just like the rest of them, but there's a gorgeous gold and green trim running across the top, adjacent to the ceiling, and all the way around the room. On the wall with the doorway, we just walked through is a small hutch with a massive mirror hanging behind it, the woodworking surrounding it as intricate as a snowflake and painted solid gold.

"Jackson, I haven't told you yet, but your house is absolutely beautiful. How do you have time to keep it up? You're already so busy as it is."

He sets the plates down on the table, and pulls out the chair next to the end for me to sit.

"I have a cleaning team. They come once a month. It's only me, so I don't make much of a mess, and I always pick up after myself." He explains, pushing my chair in after I lower into it.

He takes his own seat at the end of the table, resting on his elbows.

"I thought you said that nobody knows where you live?"

He runs his hand through his hair and shoots me a grin. "Nobody knows where Jackson Wolf lives, I registered with them under the name Scott Davis." He waves his hand dismissively in the air. "None of this *matters* right now, Olivia. *Eat,* I'm eager to see what you think." His urgency to know my thoughts sends my heart going pitter patter.

As if what I think and feel matters to him.

I oblige, twirling the noodles around my fork and stabbing a meatball.

Once I scoop the bite into my mouth, I'm stunned by how amazing it is. The sauce is tomato-ey, and tangy, and savory, and slightly sweet, and the meatballs are perfect, and the mixture together is like sex in my mouth—if I guessed what sex felt like.

"This is…" I say with a mouth full; I hold my finger up as I finish chewing and swallow. "If you don't make it in this line of work, you'd be a great chef. How did you learn to cook so well?" I shovel another scoop into my mouth as Jackson watches me. *Closely.*

"My mother and I used to cook together when I was a child, and I've continued because it's therapeutic for my hands to *create* when they've done so many things that are…unforgiveable."

My chewing slows for just a second. I want to think more and make assumptions about his mother and the rest of his family, but I decide to tuck it away to bring out later.

"Are you going to eat?" I ask and look up at him, still staring at me. I waste no time though; he stares with a particular reverence and I scoop another bite into my mouth, practically starving. I only ate a slice of pie for breakfast.

"I just…" Jackson says, and hesitates. My chewing halts and I look up at him slowly. "Since I started making the sauce this morning, I've tried to imagine all the ways you would politely tell me that it tastes like shit." My brows scrunch together and I swallow my bite, opening my mouth to object, but Jackson cuts me off. "I never imagined how *good* it would feel to see you enjoy my cooking."

My breath catches on his words. I reach for my glass to wash everything down.

I get the feeling that this is one of those times that I want to remember forever.

Once again, I open my mouth to speak, but Jackson stops me again.

"Nothing in this entire world has ever had the power to sway me, in any sense. Once my mind is set on something, that's it. Until that day on Pole Cat when you practically jumped in front of Landon." Jackson still rests on his elbows, his plate in front of him, untouched. He reaches up to run his hand through his hair and a sort of tension fills the air as he flexes his hands and rolls his neck.

"Your blind loyalty to him, the way that you risked your life to make sure that he wasn't harmed by me…it stopped me. It swayed me. I remember thinking to myself '*What a shame it would be for me to hurt this gorgeous and feisty girl. She deserves more.*' And you kept risking your life. Again, and again, and each time that I had something to do with you being okay, with being unharmed, I had this overwhelming relief. This, this…" Jackson begins to lose his words but he closes his eyes and takes a deep and calming breath.

It's a privilege to hear his innermost thoughts. His eyes stay down, at his hands that crossed together in front of him. "This weight lifted off my chest, knowing that you would be peacefully sleeping in your bed that night and breathing when you woke. It started from the moment that I saw you, Olivia."

My heart pounds away, hearing these words that seem to fill the gap of all of my moments where I felt unwanted and unworthy of somebody watching out for me.

Unworthy of someone caring for me.

"All of this to say, that I don't know where this-this…" Jackson picks his hand up to gesture between us, "will take us, but I know that I don't want it to end."

I take another sip to clear my throat and my hand reaches out for Jackson's, and I'm almost shocked when his hand wraps around mine. It's the most natural feeling in the world.

I don't want it to end, either.

I've never looked forward to something other than escaping. Than being somebody else. And being with Jackson has made me strangely…comfortable with myself. For the first time in my life, I'm hopeful—excited even—for what's to come.

There's a looming and dreary thought in the back of my mind, though. The work that he is tied up in is…dangerous. Will he continue to do what he does? Is there a retirement age on…whatever his title is?

How would that affect us? Whatever we are.

And then there's the issue of me leaving. I'm going to be leaving this town, this state, this life. I was already planning on reinventing myself after graduation, beginning to create a version of myself that I see in ten years.

A successful woman.

A powerful woman.

A strong woman.

But I'll have to give up the feelings that Jackson Wolf makes me feel in order to achieve that.

Am I really strong enough to give up the only person that's made me feel something other than loneliness and pain?

I suppose that only time will tell, but that's a problem for another day.

"Twenty-seven." I say, pulling my hand away to take another bite. I drop my eyes to my plate, waiting on his reaction, and can see his posture relax out of the corner of my eye.

Jackson picks up his own fork, the mood of the room changing in an instant.

"What makes you think that?" He asks.

I shrug, swallowing a bite and clear my throat. "Educated guess."

"Mmm." He hums, taking his first bite, finally. "Please present your factors."

I set my fork down and brush my hands together, getting ready to hold up my fingers to keep track.

"One," I hold out my index finger, "your home. It's gorgeous and planned and decorated. You've put a lot of thought into your environment. Anyone that is any younger than twenty-seven wouldn't even know to hang something like sconces in the library. Two," I add my middle finger out into the air. Jackson chews as he listens, amusement dancing in his eyes. "You are just starting to get those small creases outside of your eyes, but you're not old enough to have forehead or laugh lines." Jackson's brows raise. He brings another bite to his mouth, gesturing for me to continue.

"Three, your muscle build. Younger guys have like, their first layer of muscles, but yours are like...older. You have more layers. I'm not sure how else to explain that. Four, you say words like 'geek.'" I purse my lips and tilt my head, trying to fight my smile.

"So, therein lies my educated guess; you are twenty-seven years of age." I raise my chin as I tip my glass to him, and bring it to my lips.

Jackson only chuckles, his lashes brushing downwards. His tongue coats his lips, and in my intoxicated state, the action appears much more sensual than intended. He leans back in his chair, as relaxed as a man could be in his home.

"When I first met you, I thought that I'd never seen a man that looks like you before. Like someone cut you out of a magazine and gave you life. Someone as..." I pause, trying to think of the best word, "*attractive* as you doesn't exist in our world. We are a mediocre town with mediocre people, but when I met you, I knew that you were anything but that." Jackson watches me as I ramble, his thumb running along his bottom lip.

"From a distance, I had this image of you in my head. I'd suspected that you'd grown up far away from here, in a big city, and with parents that made decent money. A pretty, privileged boy. But..." I open my mouth to speak, and I take a few breaths. I reach for my glass and finish off the drink, setting it back down. Jackson's eyes watch me, in the way that they do, making me feel kinds of ways that would drive one mad.

"When I got up to you that first time, and I looked in your eyes, I knew that it was far from the truth. I saw someone who was tormented in some of the same ways that I was. And from that first day, I knew it in my bones, that I would see you again."

Jackson continues to run his thumb along his bottom lip for several moments, and he reaches forward for his own glass, finishing off the rest of his as well. He rises from his chair and gathers our plates and glasses.

"I'll be right back, stay right here." He commands.

I nod and sit back in the chair, a little put off that he didn't respond in any way to my pouring out my heart. I take in the scenery around me, noticing there's a door in the very corner of the room when I first entered. It's flush with the wall and pretty obscure, not noticeable in the slightest. The only indication of it being there is the small golden knob and deadbolt secured on the outside.

That's kind of suspicious.

Before I can even think another thought, Jackson steps through the door, and I whip my head around to him. He holds two more full glasses in his hands.

"I've got something for you." He starts, handing my glass to me.

My entire body is warm and tingly. How many of these drinks have I had?

"I know you're not a flashy, jewelry wearing girl. But I saw this not long ago and I just...couldn't stop thinking about seeing it around your pretty little neck." The vibrations of his purr sends goosebumps across my skin, and my knee bounces with anticipation. I take another sip and set my glass down.

He reaches for my empty hand and pulls me to my feet, bringing me around to stand in front of the mirror. It's massive, reflecting the entire dining room behind us, and showing to about where my belly button is.

"You're the only woman I've ever given a thought to, outside of a quick fuck for the night." He murmurs as I face myself and he lines up behind me. Looking at our reflection, Jackson is a solid twelve inches taller than me, his chin easily could rest on the top of my head.

His hair tumbles across his forehead as his eyes find mine in the mirror, and I notice the pink staining my cheeks from his crass words.

"You're the only woman that I've wanted to bring into my space, the only one I've wanted to see inside my home."

He lifts his hands, pulling my hair back off my shoulders and he trails his fingers down the side of my neck that is still bruised from his mouth's assault before Thanksgiving.

Those green pools of acid follow his motions, making my entire body burn. His head lowers, lips brushing the shell of my ear. "The only woman that's made me think of a different life than the one that I live. I knew when I first met you that I wouldn't be able to stay away. But I knew more than that, the moment I watched Landon kiss you at that football game. I didn't even know you. It was *insane* of me. And then when I realized you were alone with another guy at that party. The thought of him touching you, of pleasuring you, of kissing you..." He closes his eyes, pressing a small kiss below my ear. One of his hands fist the hair at the back of my neck, pulling my head slightly and giving him more access.

Watching him and I in the mirror, his lips on my neck, is the most erotic thing that I've ever seen in my life, and I think that I might be standing in a puddle by the time he's done.

"I thought that I was going to show up and kill him in front of all those kids. It was everything I could do to focus on you and you only, getting you out of there and home safely."

My body is a live wire underneath his touch. My chest rises and falls underneath his command.

"My thoughts are yours, everything about me, is yours. You've infected me, Olivia, and if you are going to be the death of me, then I'll die the happiest man on this earth." He says so low that it's almost a whisper, but much, much more sensual than that. I feel it all the way in my soul, placing every broken piece back.

His hands fall away from me and he looks at me in the mirror again, lifting his arms over my head and around front of me.

The reflection of a something shiny in the mirror makes me realize what he's doing; placing a necklace around my neck. My fingers go to touch it, and I continue to watch in the mirror as he clasps it and lifts my hair over the golden chain.

I look down, running my fingers over the pendant.

It's a golden wolf head. Encrusted with diamonds. It rests perfectly underneath the hollow of my neck, against my chest, and it just feels...*right*.

"So perfect. So mine." His fingers trail over it against my skin, leaving goosebumps in their wake.

"Thank you, Jackson. It's beautiful." I breathe.

"You're beautiful, Olivia. Absolutely breathtaking, and you don't even try. This is a reminder that you are *more* than the sun and the moon, and all the stars combined. That's what your capacity for forgiveness and love means to me." His words are enough to undo me, and before I can say or do anything else, his long fingers softly grip my jaw and he spins me slowly around to him.

"You are enough, and much more than that. Promise me that you'll remember it." He whispers as he rests his forehead against mine, his fingers still pressed against my cheeks.

I nod, breathless, unwilling to let the emotion in my chest spill out, yet.

"I will." I whisper back, our lips brushing together.

"That's my good girl." He murmurs, and catches my lips in a kiss that sends my head spinning.

Before I'm able to get too swept away in the feeling that is Jackson Wolf, he pulls away, catches his breath, and presses one more swift kiss to my lips.

"I hate to cut this short tonight, but duty calls, and I must get you home." He sounds defeated, but his eyes are bright and he has a hint of a smile on his lips when he tucks my hair behind my ears.

I can't deny the disappointment that I feel. I'm not sure what I was expecting out of tonight, but more time with him would have been a start.

A simmering jealousy bubbles in my chest, over his job. And his boss. And all the people that he's in charge of.

I hold my tongue though, grateful for the time that I did have with him tonight.

He breaks away from me, and I turn, taking one more look at the wolf head pendant hanging around my neck, feeling like I'm on top of the world.

Those looming thoughts of leaving in the fall begin to resurface, reminding me not to fall in love with a man that I won't stay with. But I snuff them out, letting myself feel just how *right* Jackson Wolf is for me.

Twenty-One

"*Oh*, no. This was not supposed to happen." I groan.

I'd asked Jackson to turn off his headlights as we came down the driveway, but my attempt to be sneaky is fruitless, as my mother rocks on the front porch in a rocking chair. A blanket is wrapped around her shoulders, and she opens her eyes when she hears us approaching.

"Are you embarrassed of me?" Jackson asks, a joking tone to his voice, but when I look to his face, I can tell from the tension framing his mouth that he is legitimately asking.

"I—I...I'm not, Jackson. It's just that my mother is a peculiar woman and I...I don't want her to scare you off." The words tumble out from me, but they don't feel sturdy enough to be a reason for my sudden panic.

I've never had a boyfriend for my mother to meet. One time she told me that any boy or man that gets stuck with me would be an idiot. A great thing for a young girl at the ripe age of fourteen to hear. It made me feel even more unworthy of any kind of male attention. I did everything I could to not be bothered by a boy so I didn't even have to think about my appearance or stupid things like the way I eat or the clothes I wear.

"Well, it's not like she will be around for much longer to change my mind about you." He says, his tone a little clipped.

My head snaps to him, almost speechless. I'm not an idiot. I know that he doesn't like my mother, but that comment was a little insensitive.

"Excuse me?"

Jackson sighs, his lashes casting down, shielding his eyes as he grips the gear-shift. "Bad form. I just got the feeling that you wouldn't want to bring me home to mom. I'm sorry."

That one sentence makes me remember that Jackson has his own issues that he works through. Some of them are adjacent to mine. I know how it feels for someone to be embarrassed by me.

I never want to make him feel that way.

So, I lean over the console when he fully parks the vehicle, and don't care one bit that my mother is sitting on the front porch, looking out at us.

It's pitch-black outside, she can't see anything.

My hand rests on his stubbled cheek and I press a kiss against his lips, my own still tingling from our interaction at his house before we left. I decide to take a page from Jackson's playbook and run my tongue along his bottom lip.

But the reaction that I get in return, is not what I was expecting.

A deep, throaty groan emits from Jackson's chest and he reaches over, grips my leg, and pulls me across the console, completely straddling his lap.

A shriek escapes at the sudden and quick motion, but my breath is completely gone when he places his large hands on my hips and he grinds up against me.

"Jackson," I whisper out, almost in a moan, when that one simple action—paired with the twin flames peering at me— stokes that fire that I'd only just put out before we got in the car.

One of his hands slide up my side and around my back, delving into the hair at the nape of my neck. He pulls me down to him, latching his lips onto mine.

He kisses me with the urgency of a starving man that hadn't eaten in days, and I'm more than willing to be his sustenance.

"Kiss me like that again," Jackson mumbles as he breaks our kiss, and grinds against me again, eliciting another breathy moan, "and I don't know if I'll be able to stop myself from fucking you right here, right now, Olivia."

I gasp against his lips at his filthy words, unable to deny the effect that they have on me. A hot and wet need spreads throughout the very center of me and one more thrust upwards against me is enough to make me collapse.

"But not tonight, baby." He whispers and captures my lips once more, his hands roaming back to my hips and giving them a squeeze.

A disappointment replaces the anticipation that bubbled in my belly and I run my fingers through his hair, placing another kiss against his soft lips.

"My mother is waiting." I whisper back, almost in agreeance. I'm reluctant though, to leave the bubble that's comprised of only him and I.

"Then let's put a face to the bad boy that left a hickey on your neck." He grins, a whisper of mischief dancing in his eyes.

I cross back over console to the passenger and yelp when a large hand smacks against my ass.

"Jackson!" I huff when I get back into the seat.

"Oh, yeah. You're ready now."

"Why did you do that?!" I brush my hair from my face and look at him with wide eyes.

"I had to make sure you were good and flustered. Mommy needs to know I'm taking care of her little girl." He says sarcastically and leans over to kiss me swiftly, still in a playful mood, but his words resonate somewhere deep in my heart. I've never needed someone to take care of me, except in the basic sense of me being a child.

But the thought of wanting someone to take care of me in every other way sounds…nice. And it sounds like things wouldn't be so heavy all the time.

It sounds like home.

"Let's go, weirdo." I roll my eyes, but can't hide the smile playing at my lips.

We both exit his vehicle and walk the short distance to the steps of the front porch, silently. My nerves tumble around my belly like a ping-pong in one of those arcade games.

I don't know exactly why my mother meeting Jackson scares the hell out of me, but they just seem like an unlikely match.

My mother is the bitchiest bitch I've ever met, and Jackson could squash her like a mosquito. Not that he would, or have any reason to, other than the unsavory comments that he's made about her being a bad mother.

Just from his demeanor when I talk about her, I know that he isn't a fan. Jackson was maddeningly quiet when I first met him, only staring at me with those intense green eyes. Since, though, he's opened up, and he speaks to me like any other person.

I've not ever seen him in a situation like this, where I would really like him to be on his best behavior. I only hope that he will be.

"Hey, Mom. What are you doing out here?" I ask when we step up onto the porch. She lifts her head and smiles weakly, tugging the blanket back up onto her shoulders.

"I'm just enjoying the evening air. It's been a long time since I've sat on this front porch and rocked, alone with my thoughts." She croaks out.

"I see." I say. Jackson's comforting touch reaches the small of my back and I breathe in. "This is Jackson, Jackson this is my mother."

"Ahh, the delicious smelling man." She says and my eyes go wide. Jackson snickers next to me and pats my back softly.

"Mom!" I scold.

"What? I'm dying, I'm allowed to say what I want. How are you, Jackson? It's so nice to meet the man that finally made my daughter think about something other than school and work." She softly rocks, and Jackson looks at me with a grin.

"The pleasure is all mine, Ms...."

"Hayes, Allison Hayes." She finishes for him.

"Ms. Allison Hayes. Your daughter has done much more for me, I can assure you. She's incredible." He says with much more emotion in his voice than I can handle for this particular meeting. My mother smiles softly, gratifyingly.

A ringing comes from Jackson's pocket and he fishes it out to look at the screen.

"And that, is my queue." He turns to me with an apologetic smile as he reaches up to stroke the line of my jaw. "I have to get going. I'll be out of town for a few days, but I'll come see you as soon as I'm back." He says and places a kiss against my forehead.

I try not to huff out my annoyance for him being out of town. He's a grown man, he has to make a living.

"And it was so nice meeting you, Ms. Allison. I hope you see you when I get back." He tells her, and I can't tell if he's being facetious or not.

"Lord willing, you will. Have a safe trip, Jackson." She tells him, and he breaks away from me, taking the short trek back to his car parked behind mine.

He drives off and I settle into the chair next to my mother. I can hear her shallow, rattling breaths as she takes them.

"He is handsome, Lottie." She says softly, her head resting against the chair.

"He is." I agree, pulling my knees up to my chest.

"He seems...dangerous, Lottie." She warns, softly again.

I don't meet her stare, yet. I look out from underneath the roof over the porch and see the stars, and I think about Jackson's words.

"This is just a reminder that you are more than the sun and the moon, and all the stars combined."

My chest rises and falls, fully feeling the emotions swimming behind my ribcage.

"He is." I agree, but not in the way that she thinks.

Jackson Wolf is definitely dangerous, but he'd never be dangerous to me. I've felt it in his touch, and his kiss, and the looks he gives me.

"You are happy." She states, and I finally direct my gaze to her.

"I am." I smile softly and reach out for her hand.

She reciprocates and squeezes my fingers softly. "That's all that matters, sweetheart. I love you more than I can say, and I know that one day you'll know what I mean when you have your own babies."

Talk of my own children gives me a strange feeling and I try to deflect, not wanting to get into any awkward conversation. Kids are not something even remotely close to anything that's on my list of things to do in the next *ten years.*

"Do you need help inside?" I ask her as I stand, stretching my arms above my head.

She pulls her blanket back over her shoulder and she shakes her head.

"I think I'm going to stay out here for a little while longer. Get some rest, baby. I love you."

"I—I love you, Mom." I tell her, and I truly mean it for the first time in my life. I reach down to give her a hug, careful not to hurt her, and I pull away before the tears in my eyes spill over my cheeks.

I leave her there, with a heavy weight sitting on my chest. My steps are like lead, reluctant to leave her sitting on the porch.

Don't go.

But I force myself. One foot in front of the other. I head up to my room to shower and prepare for bed.

CHAPTER

Twenty-Two

*A*s a young girl, I remember that I felt like I wouldn't be upset if my mother were to suddenly pass away. She was against everything about me. Her mere existence chafed mine. I remember that I'd hoped it would happen swiftly, a piano dropping from the sky, or a train coming out of nowhere. I knew that I would be fine because I would end up living with Nana.

I thought it would be easier than this.

I thought that I wouldn't feel a thing. She'd be breathing. Then she'd be gone. And I would be *better*.

Expect the unexpected, they say. I'd always *prayed* for the unexpected.

Until now.

I knew.

I knew that she was going to die.

I knew that her cancer was advanced and we wouldn't get much time with her.

However, I figured we'd get longer than a week. I thought that I would have more time to heal and forgive and replace the bad memories with the few short good ones we'd be able to make up.

I was *wrong.*

Never in my life will I forget the scream that woke me up this morning. Never, ever, will I forget that I was nauseous before my head even left the pillow.

Last night, she was rocking peacefully.

This morning, *she's gone.*

As soon as I heard Nana's guttural cry for help from the Lord, Himself, I was on my feet and racing down the steps before I could even properly open my eyes.

She was nowhere in the house that I could see, and I realized that she was on the front porch.

Resting serenely, right where I left her last night.

Before I even set eyes on her, my world shifted on its axis.

Everything was different.

Yet, everything was the same.

The wind blew softly in the early morning light, the dew wet against the grass. The fog hadn't even cleared from the pastures yet.

Everything was the same.

The birds were singing.

The sun was rising.

The breeze was bristling the leaves in the pines.

Everything was just like any other morning.

And, yet…*everything was different.*

My mother had finally lost her battle, and she did so peacefully, rocking in that fucking chair that I left her in.

When I finally stepped onto the front porch, Nana was cradling my mother in her lap on the wooden floor.

She rocked back and forth, her agonizing wails slicing through my chest each time I heard them.

We knew this was coming. We knew what the outcome would be.

But it doesn't hurt any fucking less.

I dropped to my knees next to Nana, wrapping my arms around her shoulders, and I forced myself to look at my mother, even though the ache in my chest was one that I couldn't rub away.

Her skin was still yellow, her extremities, like her fingers and lips, had already turned blue. Her eyes were closed and her mouth was relaxed. She looked like she was sleeping.

She was peaceful.

She was out of pain.

And she was gone.

CHAPTER

Twenty-Three

Fuck.

CHAPTER

Twenty-Four

*D*ecember 2nd.

It's been a week since my mother died. The first day was practically unbearable. The second was hard, too. I didn't feel as blown apart as I did when Landon died, though, given that his was so unexpected. The third day, that Monday, Nana and I picked up her ashes from the funeral home and drove to a little pond that sits on the edge of our property, and spread her ashes around.

She'd loved water, she wanted to live and die on the beach.

Instead, she got the front porch of her mother's home in Shit-hole Chiefland, Florida.

I used to love this town, and now it's stained and tainted.

I should have taken her to the coast and stayed with her until she passed instead of leaving her on the front porch to die cold and alone.

I knew it when I walked away from her. I felt it. That invisible force telling me that I shouldn't leave her.

I stayed home from school this week; my teachers being immensely understanding about the situation.

I've called Jackson one hundred times.

Voicemail.

One hundred times.

In a time like this.

I'm trying to be as strong as I can and him not answering is making me think the absolute worst.

Is he okay?

Is he dead, too?

Will he come back to me?

He spoke to me as if I were important to him. He whispered words in my ear that I've never heard, and he pushed me over that abyss, falling.

Falling for him.

Falling for his touch.

Falling for his mind and his words and the lips that spoke them.

Falling for the green eyes that could see *me* without uttering a single word.

Falling for the tall, dark, and dangerous man, especially when he was soft, and sensitive, passionate.

And now, it's like he never existed. The only things I have of him are the things he'd gifted me. I don't even know how to get to his home.

I'm not much of a religious person anymore, but I pray, to all things holy, that he is okay, and that he comes back.

The stronger side of me, the one that shut out my mother for so long and wished for her death, tells me that it doesn't matter if he comes back, and if he hasn't yet, then good fucking riddance.

I am leaving in the fall anyways. I shouldn't be concerned with the whims of grown men that play with knives and are involved with my best friend's death.

No, I must have something different.

I have aspirations.

I have dreams.

I have plans.

And none of them involved a dark-haired, green-eyed, gorgeous man that makes my toes curl.

Tonight, Sadie and her parents invited Nana and me to a Christmas party. Nana opted not to go, being that she hasn't gone anywhere or done anything since we spread my mother's ashes in the pond. She even caved and hired a farmhand to help her indefinitely.

But, me, on the other hand, I have to go to the party. Despite the open wound in my chest that feels a lot like a festering sore, I have to get out of this house. I need to stop worrying about Jackson, and stop thinking about the time I never got with my mother, and stop wondering about my father and uncle and twin brother—the only family that I might still have.

Sadie let me pick out a dress out of her closet to wear. It's a strange coincidence that she had the most gorgeous dark green dress. Its sleeves are lace, and it has a deep plunging cut-out in the valley between my breasts, exposing just enough. It's tighter around my middle and hangs looser around my feet.

It's really beautiful, tighter and cinched in just the right places, accentuating the more savory parts of me.

Loose curls hang in my dark brown hair down my back and around my waist. A small bit of concealer takes away the dark circles and pale skin from days of crying. A dab of blush gives me more color, bringing me back to life. A tinted lip-gloss coats my lips, making them plumper and pinker. I have some golden flats that I had in my closet and the dress covers them, anyways.

If it weren't so hard to breathe lately, I might actually call myself a knock out as I look at myself in the mirror.

The hickey has finally faded, but strangely...I miss his mark on my skin. The only thing on my neck is the diamond encrusted wolf head pendant. It compliments my skin tone in the most perfect way, and I wish I knew what Jackson would say if he saw me wearing it with this outfit.

"You look beautiful, Liv." Sadie says as she steps up to me, locking her arm around mine.

"Me? Look at you. You're a real-life Barbie." I say dryly, but Sadie laughs it off.

Sadie's blonde hair has grown a bit, down to her shoulders, and she has it curled in loose waves. She opted to wear a golden dress that has one strap over the shoulder and one full golden sleeve down the other. It's form fitting until her waist and then it flows, its length touching the floor.

"Are you ready to go eat some fancy food?" She grins at me in the mirror.

I nod in response and touch her arm around mine, grateful for the person standing next to me through all of this. Despite the pain that hasn't let up in the slightest.

Prime & Pearl is an extravagant restaurant in Gainesville, Florida. Located about forty miles away, it's the nicest eatery in the tri-county area. Sure, there's small, hole-in-the-wall places that are cute and cozy and the food probably easily rivals the expensive one.

But they have eight courses and you can only purchase alcohol by buying the bottle, and by the time you leave, the bill is $300 for two people...and that's barley eating any food. So, naturally, people flock to it.

I, myself, would never choose to eat at a place like this, not while I'm trying to save up money for my new start. But when someone else is paying for it?

Don't mind if I do.

It gives me a chance to play dress up and pretend to be somebody else for the night.

Tonight, I'm not Olivia Charlotte Hayes.

Tonight, I'm Olivia Literally-Anyone-Else Hayes.

And that straightens my back bone a little bit as I walk through the massive double doors being held by waiters in black suits and black ties.

I walk in with my head held high, knowing that one day, when I make something of myself, I will be attending places like this.

Simply because I can, and I want to.

There are chandeliers and round tables with white table clothes and waiters carrying around trays with bottles of champagne in buckets of ice and the food smells…really good.

The lighting is super romantic, but still bright enough to see everyone clearly.

Sadie and I, arm in arm, follow behind her parents as the hostess leads us through the crowd and the rows of tables. We are shown to our seats, which is one table of the five reserved ones in an entire corner of the restaurant. I think Sadie's mother said these are her coworkers on the drive over.

Sadie and I exchange excited glances as we take in the scenery and enjoy the real-life tea party.

I try to shove my loss and my grief and my worry and my tears behind that door, hoping that at least tonight, just for tonight, I can get a breath amidst the suffocation of the constant agony that I've felt for the last week.

So, I talk.

And smile.

And laugh.

And act interested.

Even if it's all an act.

The waiter brings us our drinks, and then our soups. Appetizers follow, and then our salads, and meal. We work through the courses, and before we can make it to dessert, I realize that I've got to use the restroom. Probably due to the four…or five glasses of champagne that I've downed.

"Hey, Sadie," I lean over, my words a little slow and my eyes feeling a little heavy. "I have to use the bathroom. I'll be right back."

She smiles and says, "Okay!"

I stand to my feet and straighten out my dress around me, looking around to find the bathrooms.

It's easy, they are right on the corner adjacent to ours. I step out and begin the trek around our table. I take a few steps out of the crowd and around the corner. From here, it's a straight shot.

No more than twenty feet from where I start the journey, I end up right in front of the bathroom door. I reach for the handle but stop and take in my surroundings for a moment.

To my left is the kitchen.

To my right is a private room.

There's nobody behind me so I take a couple glances at the private room.

Suits. Suits. Private bar. Private waiters. Half-naked girls.

Privileged ass fuckers.

I go to roll my eyes and tug on the bathroom door handle, when something stops me in my tracks.

I lock eyes with a man.

A gorgeous one.

With dark, tousled, hair.

And a pair of green eyes that captivate me, like fucking magic.

And on his lap, sits a skinny, lingerie-clad, red-haired, perfectly-pouted lips *model.*

While my entire world is turning upside down, *again,* Jackson Wolf stares back at me, devoid of emotion.

As if I were a stranger on the street.

As if I were *nothing.*

His eyes rake down the front of my dress, as if I were there just for his perusal, and he turns his head to whisper into the ear of the bitch perched on his lap, his hand sliding up her thigh-high fishnets.

No.

So many questions pour into my head so quickly that stars cloud my vision, and I back away.

One step.

Breathe in.

Another step.

Breathe out.

Don't run. Don't make a scene.

Breathe in.

Another step.

Breathe out.

I turn in my place and I continue those steps back toward the way we came.

Breathe in.

Don't look at anyone. *Get the fuck out of here before you break, Olivia.* Just go.

Breathe out.

Past Sadie. Past the hostess stand. To the doors.

Breathe in.

Push the doors, Olivia, go. *Go.* Hold on just a second longer. *Please.*

Breathe out.

The second that I exit the doors and step outside, ice-cold pelting rain drenches my hair, my face, my dress, soaking into my skin immediately.

Soaking into my soul.

The opening chasm in my chest suddenly reminds me of why I began to find solace in being alone. Because I never, *ever,* wanted to know this kind of guttural, raw pain.

The thing is, though, is that life never gives a shit about anything that you want.

And more so, *never, ever* anything that you need.

AUTHOR'S NOTE

Dear Reader,

None of this would be possible without you. I hope you enjoyed the beginning of Olivia and Jackson's journey, as much as I've enjoyed bringing it to life. Don't worry, this isn't the end of Olivia Hayes and Jackson Wolf. There will be more.

The next page has a list of songs that I feel really captures the vibe for *Chasing Shadows*.

Be on the look-out for the next addition to *Chasing Shadows*...

Enjoy!

Elizabeth

PLAYLIST

Heathens – Twenty One Pilots

This – Ed Sheeran

Broken – lovelytheband

Afire Love – Ed Sheeran

Gravity – John Mayer

Make It Rain – Ed Sheeran

Say Something – A Great Big World & Christina Aguilera

CATCHING SILHOUETTES

(Book 2)

Following the death of her best friend and her mother, and the betrayal by her (almost) lover, Olivia Hayes must learn how to navigate life after high school with the looming threat of her family's empire catching up to her.

She fights, and she loves, and she plots, and she finds that life isn't always what it may seem at first glance.

However, all good things must come to an end.

And not all endings are good.